"Just tell me. Did you kill someone?"

Allie searched Dal's face. But all she saw was
the tense expression of a man caught in the grip
of an inner torment. His pale green eyes were
narrowed and bright with tension. She swallowed.
"What happened?"

Dal met her gaze squarely. "No questions. Either
you want me here or you don't."

A long silence stretched between them while Allie
considered what had been said, and what she knew
of Dal. The decision was a matter of faith, and Dal
had always seemed trustworthy. She faced him
squarely. "I want you to stay. I need you. You're
a godsend."

Instead of relaxing, Dal's features hardened until his
frown was fierce. He turned away, and whistled up
his gelding. His words were angry as he rode off.
"I'm *nobody's* godsend, hear? The minute you start
relying on me, I'll be gone."

Dear Reader,

During this holiday season, as friends and loved ones gather for Thanksgiving, Silhouette Romance is celebrating all the joys of family and, of course, romance!

Each month in 1992, as part of our WRITTEN IN THE STARS series, we're proud to present a Silhouette Romance that focuses on the hero and his astrological sign. This month we're featuring sexy Scorpio Luke Manning. You may remember Luke as the jilted fiancé from Kasey Michaels's *Lion on the Prowl.* In *Prenuptial Agreement,* Luke finds true love...right in his own backyard.

We have an extra reason to celebrate this month—Stella Bagwell's HEARTLAND HOLIDAYS trilogy. In *Their First Thanksgiving,* Sam Gallagher meets his match when Olivia Westcott returns to the family's Arkansas farm. She'd turned down Sam's proposal once, but he wasn't about to let her go this time.

To round out the month we have warm, wonderful love stories from Anne Peters, Kate Bradley, Patti Standard– and another heart-stopping cowboy from Dorsey Kelley.

In the months to come, watch for Silhouette Romance novels by many more of your favorite authors, including Diana Palmer, Annette Broadrick, Elizabeth August and Marie Ferrarella.

The Silhouette authors and editors love to hear from readers, and we'd love to hear from *you.*

Happy reading from all of us at Silhouette!

Valerie Susan Hayward
Senior Editor

TEXAS MAVERICK
Dorsey Kelley

Silhouette
R O M A N C E™
Published by Silhouette Books New York
America's Publisher of Contemporary Romance

To my friends at the Rankin Ranch.
Thank you for your generous time, patience and enthusiasm, as well as the fun!

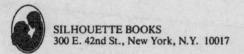

SILHOUETTE BOOKS
300 E. 42nd St., New York, N.Y. 10017

TEXAS MAVERICK

ISBN: 0-373-08900-7

First Silhouette Books printing November 1992

Printed in the U.S.A.

Books by Dorsey Kelley

Silhouette Romance

Montana Heat #714
Lone Star Man #863
Texas Maverick #900

DORSEY KELLEY

claims she has loved and read romance novels forever and can't bear to throw one away. Hence—books stuck into every cranny of her house. Her interests include romping with her three small daughters, tennis and a good bottle of champagne shared with her husband. She lives near the coast in Southern California.

MAVERICK

An unbranded animal; independent

A man no woman could brand

Chapter One

The cowboy rode in from the west.

The setting sun was hard on his back, forcing Allie to shade her eyes and squint through the glare to make him out. A dark-haired man on an enormous horse, he appeared to be in no hurry to reach the front gate of her small, Texas Panhandle ranch.

Allie willed herself to wait patiently, when all she wanted to do was run out and grab him. She didn't know him, of course, had never met him. For all she knew he could be a salesman, a lost soul asking directions or even a rustler.

No. He was a working man—Allie recognized that from twenty paces. And she knew he'd come to answer her ad. An ad she'd run several times with no response, because what she could afford to pay made even the old-timers down at Carson's drugstore howl and slap their thighs.

Feminine intuition whispered insistently that the man who sat his saddle with inbred grace and wore his black Stetson pulled low was the answer to all her problems. For some inexplicable reason, Allie was convinced: God had sent her a miracle in the form of a man.

Not that she was interested in him personally. There was far too much at stake to take more than cursory notice of the confident, almost cocky set of his wide shoulders, his big hands steady and sure on the leather reins or his long, muscled thighs clamped about the gleaming night-dark gelding. It didn't matter to her in the least if his deeply tanned face held features of pleasing masculine symmetry—a lean jaw, straight bold nose and arresting, black-fringed eyes.

What mattered to Allie was that he was big and strong and obviously able to withstand, even thrive under, the back-breaking labor of a small, family-run cow-calf operation. A family whose numbers had dwindled to herself and Jessie.

With narrowed, assessing eyes, she studied the man's thickened, blunt-tipped fingers, made so by hard work. She noted the battered condition of his hat, weathered by long winters and summers of constant wear. His jeans were faded and his chaps marked by too-close brushes with barbed-wire fences.

"Ma'am." The big man reined his horse to a halt just outside the gate and tipped his hat.

"Need work?" she asked, not moving from her post on the dilapidated front porch, although a voice inside urged her to drag him inside and bar the gate.

"I'd appreciate it." He glanced around, his gaze wandering over the front yard with its pile of spare tires and rusted equipment, to the rose garden from which Allie's mother had once coaxed cheerful blossoms, where now grew only thorny, dried-up stalks. Allie cringed inwardly as the stranger's expressionless gaze drifted past her old rattletrap car, whose muffler was tied up with baling wire, and on to the big barn with its peeling paint.

"We can't pay much," she blurted, aware that her tone was abrupt, but unable to help it. "But you'll get three squares and the bunkhouse to yourself." With a nail-bitten index finger, she indicated a small structure opposite the barn. "And you'll be plenty busy. We can't abide loafers here."

He regarded her without blinking: a direct, bottomless inspection that touched her lightly. There was no censure, yet he missed nothing. Not her ragged jeans and smudged white T-shirt advertising bottled beer, nor her plain hip-length braid the color of summer hayfields.

She hated how she must appear, hated what he inevitably saw, a dirt-poor, flea-bitten spread in the middle of Nowhere, Texas, and a half-desperate woman in dire need of a man.

A man to work the ranch, of course.

Her back stiffened automatically and her lips firmed. Years ago she had been carefree, and even now her temperament was usually sunny, although less so lately. She couldn't afford to be carefree anymore. "Put your horse in the barn," she told him. "There's grain and hay. When you're done, come on up to the house, supper's almost ready." In cool dismissal, she turned her back.

"Ma'am?"

"Yes?" She jerked around, her fingers unconsciously gripping the silver belt buckle strapped to her waist, her only remaining possession of value.

"Name's Dal."

One fair brow raised. Unusual, but it was his ability to work that she cared about. He could be Joe or Slim or Frank for all it mattered. "Dal what?"

"Just Dal. You're ... ?"

"Allie Pearson. I'll go check on supper." With that unsubtle reminder to hurry, she strode into the house, her worn-down boot heels making a sharp echo on the unstable boards.

At the kitchen counter she finished putting together the simple meal of fried hamburgers and a bowl of sliced melon. As she set out buns and other fixings on the scarred wooden table, she cast a fond eye over her daughter. It had been difficult taking over the ranch this year since her parents had died. Nothing seemed to go right, and raising little Jessie alone was difficult, too. She needed constant attention and love, and Allie was often divided between work and her daughter. At times it hurt that she couldn't give Jess, a bright light in her life, all the attention the girl deserved. There was always so much to do!

Jessie came into the kitchen and sat at the table, her four-year-old legs dangling in cotton pants two inches too short. "Mommy, can I pour milk? Please? Please?"

Feeling her frown ease, Allie smiled. "Sure, sweetie. But do it slowly like Mommy showed you. No spilling."

"I will!" Excited with this adult responsibility, the girl hopped down, raced to the refrigerator, threw open the door so hard it crashed against the wall and grabbed for the plastic container. It tipped, sending a flood of milk over the inside of the fridge and across the floor.

Allie sighed.

"I'm sorry." Jessie's huge blue eyes, so like her mother's, filled and she put three fingers in her mouth. Against her small chest a long dark braid trembled with suppressed sobs.

Allie tamped down her frustration and tried not to think about the price of milk. She knelt beside Jessie and cuddled her close. "It was an accident. We don't want that old milk tonight, anyway, do we? Let's have apple juice. I'll pour."

Jessie smiled through her tears, and Allie bent to the floor with a sponge. While she wiped, the girl ran into the adjoining living room and skidded to a halt before the front door. "Mister, I spilled milk *everywhere*." She announced her news grandly.

In the doorway stood the stranger.

"Uh, come in." Allie straightened, gestured awkwardly as she moved to the sink to squeeze out the milk. She'd known he was large, even on his horse she could see that. But now that he stood before her with cool nonchalance, he seemed to fill up the room. She guessed six-four, two-twenty, and swallowed hard. The man was as big as a barn.

"Jess," she said, "this is the new hand I hired on. His name is Dal."

Allie said to the stranger, "This is my daughter, Jessie."

Dal nodded, silent. He waited.

"You can wash up in there." She pointed toward the front bathroom.

"I'll show you!" Jessie cried, hurling her little body headlong down the hallway to point out the room. Instead of exhibiting a normal shyness with strangers, Jessie usually marched right up to them and demanded their name. After that, she would bombard them with the latest happenings in her small world. Allie shook her head ruefully, hoping Jessie would outgrow some of that. She'd have to become more wary to survive.

When Dal emerged from the bathroom, he placed his sheepskin jacket on a peg by the door and hung his hat beside it. Allie noticed his raven-black hair was damp, as if he'd scrubbed behind his ears like a boy taught by a conscientious mother. She wondered at his background.

"Are you hungry?" she asked.

His dark-fringed eyes slid over to the plate of burgers with a covetous gleam, and she supposed an out-of-work cowboy might hardly know where his next meal was coming from. She was glad she'd made plenty.

"Real hungry," he replied.

"Good." She pointed to a chair. "Sit."

Without ceremony the three took seats at the table and dug into the burgers.

Dal said little, merely ate methodically while Jessie chattered about how she was going to save all her pennies and buy herself a real live pony.

"And he'll be big and have black and white spots all over," she told the table at large. "Then I can go on round-ups with Mommy."

Allie caught Dal's surprised glance at this. She knew what he was thinking and mentally shrugged. If he couldn't handle the idea of a woman doing men's work, he'd best light out right now. To his credit, he said nothing.

"I think you should know what you're in for," Allie told Dal without preamble. Beneath his faded, brown, long-sleeved shirt his shoulders were wide, tapering to a flat belly and long legs. Allie blinked nervously, then wondered at her unease. He was just a cowboy, for goodness' sake. She went on. "We're running several hundred head of Herefords and doing it ourselves. For help we have only Pete, a high school boy who comes out after school and on weekends. Cattle prices are down, the drought's drying us up, and we took big chances by buying three new bulls last June."

Dal wiped his mouth and chewed thoughtfully. "Are most of the cows settled?"

"Yes. I think we'll have our first calving early, about February—in two weeks. If we don't get any cold snaps, and if we get a good live calf crop, we'll be okay." Left unsaid were a lot more *ifs*.

"I'll ride out tomorrow and have a look at them."

Allie nodded. She was relieved he wasn't scared off by her little speech. "We're winter feeding now because with the lack of water, range conditions aren't good. That'll be one of your everyday chores—taking the pickup out to the pastures with hay and cottonseed cake. There's plenty around here for me to do without that job."

"How many good cow horses do you have?" he asked.

In her chair she shifted uncomfortably. "Well, most have been running on the range all year. I haven't been able to bring them in. They need to be saddle-broke again."

Dal stared at her without blinking. But Allie could sense his shock. Breaking and retraining the seven to nine good horses he'd need was a big job. She hurried on. "Besides that, there's post holes to be dug, wire to be strung, windmills that need repair. As I told you before, a lot of work."

Dal shrugged his big shoulders under his faded shirt. "I like to keep busy."

She picked up her burger, took a small bite and swallowed. For the first time she allowed herself to smile at him. "Then you'll be very happy here."

He studied her face with an unwavering, sober inspection that doubled her unease, and her smile faded. She wasn't afraid of him, exactly. What she felt now was something else—something alien she couldn't identify.

Suddenly she found herself hoping there was no catsup at the corner of her mouth, hoping her braid was smooth and wishing she'd applied mascara to her ridiculously light eyelashes.

Finishing his last bite, Dal said, "Why don't you show me the grounds?"

"All right," she said slowly, thrown off guard. When Jessie ran to the television and turned on cartoons, she shrugged. Now was as good a time as any.

Outside, the sun had disappeared behind the low horizon and the crickets had started singing. It was even cooler now, so Allie grabbed her father's old denim jacket and put it on for warmth. She was halfway down the steps when Dal's voice stopped her. Instead of following her, he leaned against the porch rail and crossed his arms. "You're running this spread alone, aren't you?"

She stopped, each foot on a different riser. "So?"

"It's too much."

"I beg your pardon?"

"It's too much work for a big man, much less one small woman. What do you do with the kid while you're tending cattle?"

"The *kid* goes with me. At least, when it's possible, if it's any of your business."

"Where's her dad?"

Presenting him with her profile, Allie crossed her arms beneath her breasts. "He doesn't live with us. He's, uh...gone."

"Gone?"

"Dead. He's dead, all right?"

"Dead, huh?" Dal's eyes narrowed, as if he could tell she was lying, though he couldn't possibly know. Softly he asked, "You don't wear his ring anymore, either? Where's he buried?"

Allie whirled on him. "Why all the questions? It's none of your damn business, Dal...whatever your last name is! All that should concern you is that you're hired to work this ranch."

"Just one more question."

"No!"

"Why don't you sell out? Buy a little place in town. This spread's falling apart. In town the life sure would be easier. And your kid could go to school—"

"*Sell out!* I wouldn't even consider it. Not in a million years. And our ranch will belong to my family long after you're gone." She forced herself to calm, but her voice was still tight with outrage. "I don't expect you to understand. You've obviously never owned any property—worked your *own* spread. You can't possibly comprehend..." She trailed off, amazed at herself. Why was she explaining anything to this—this apparently shiftless bumpkin?

But she caught a fleeting expression cross his face, a deep sorrow mingled with helpless frustration. And she noticed he was fingering something that hung on a chain around his neck. It was tarnished and appeared to be a sort of medallion.

When he glanced up and caught her looking, he put it back inside his shirt with a deliberate movement. "Think I'll turn in, if it's okay with you, boss." His tone held neither sarcasm nor criticism, yet she sensed both. "I'll check out the grounds tomorrow."

"Suit yourself." She wanted to say more—tell him that if he was going to stick his nose into her personal business, he could saddle up and ride right out.

But she didn't. Because even if Dal turned out to be the nosiest cowhand in the West, she couldn't afford to let him go. She was desperate, she reminded herself stoically. And he was here, willing and able to work. She needed him.

For the next four days Dal worked and rode the ranch and wondered what the hell Allie Pearson thought she was doing. Nothing escaped his notice. Although clean, the barn needed painting. The fences had to be a good thirty or forty years old with brittle rusted wire and rotten fence posts that could hardly hold a staple; whole sections needed to be scrapped and replaced. The windmills had never been updated—made of wood instead of modern galvanized angle iron—and were dangerous to climb. He never knew when the wood he was standing on might turn into daylight.

Even though it was winter the flies were harassing the cattle, causing irritation which usually led to less weight gain—which translated into less profit come shipping day. Dal shrugged and brought the most agitated to a corral close to the barn for treatment. Shaking his head, he squinted from under his hat toward the house.

Allie was throwing leftover corn cobs into the chicken coop where she kept several dozen laying hens. She was always busy, hard at work, and she did seem to take her daughter with her everywhere.

Against his will and even his better judgment he wondered about little Jessie's father. He guessed he was a good enough judge of character to recognize a basically honest woman when he saw one. The trouble with basically honest people was they made cussed poor liars.

The woman knew something of ranching—but not enough. The place was sadly rundown, and unless she had some outside money to bring in, which he doubted, it was only a matter of time before the bank owned one more piece of scrub oak, mediocre cattle and lost dreams.

She was fighting a losing battle. Even if he *could* do anything about it, he wouldn't. He wasn't any kind of rescuer, just the opposite. He let people down.

Without warning, the harsh dissonant sound of gunshots echoed in his memory—the sight of blood—the smell of death. Dal squeezed his eyes shut and gritted his teeth against the agonizing images.

Sweat gathered on his brow and slipped down his shirt collar. His fists clenched and his breathing grew ragged.

Two years. Two long years he'd lived and relived the scene until he was afraid he'd go mad with it. Maybe he already had.

Shaken, Dal opened his eyes and felt the familiar bleakness steal over his soul, leaving only bitter frustration and shame. Self-loathing clawed at him as he guided his black gelding toward the farthest pasture and away from the woman.

He would scratch out a living with only the strength of his back and the skill of his hands with lariat and hammer. It was enough now—it had to be. He had nothing left to give.

"What do you want, Jed?" Allie demanded of the disreputable man who hung over the half-rotted boards of her front gate. "I thought I told you to get out and stay out."

"You did, Miz Pearson," the thin man in a slouch hat agreed. He scratched his sallow cheek with one dirty fingernail. "That you did. But y'see, there's the matter of my pay. You owe me a hundred dollars."

"No." She shook her head. "You owe *me*. You spent, more days sleeping off drunks in the bunkhouse than you ever put in on horseback. In fact, in one of your drunks, you fell over this gate and broke it." She rattled the hinge to demonstrate the broken latch. "Furthermore, you left Sally still saddled and sweaty outside the barn after you pushed her too hard, and she foundered. I had to pay the vet double for a Sunday visit!" With this she leaned forward and her anger caused her voice to deepen. "I know you took those twenties I had in the cookie jar, Jed, though I can't prove it. The boys in town told me you showed up with gambling money last Saturday night."

During Allie's tirade, Jed's wheedling smile transformed into a sullen mask. "I worked for you, Miz Pearson. I aim to get paid." With an aggressive motion, he slapped his hand over hers.

She tried—and failed—to snatch it away just as Dal walked up behind her.

"I suggest you let the lady go, amigo, and head out while the atmosphere's still friendly." Dal's tone was soft, almost gentle, yet his expression was anything but.

Jed glanced up at the big man with open-mouthed surprise. He took his hand away from Allie's but didn't back down. "You the new man around here? Well, it don't mat-

ter. This is business between the lady boss and me. When I
get my hundred bucks, I'll go.''

Shouldering her aside, Dal tipped back his hat and placed
his big hand exactly where Jed's had been on the gate. Beneath his grip, Allie heard the wood crack. Her initial ap-
prehension at seeing the troublemaking Jed again increased
in the face of Dal's menacing manner. His low voice
dropped even lower. "Maybe you didn't understand. I'll put
it this way—it's no longer *healthy* for you around here,
savvy?''

"Yeah. Sure.'' Jed took new stock of his position and
made a belated decision to take four quick steps back. For
the tenth time Allie congratulated herself for hiring Dal.
He'd proven knowledgeable and capable around the ranch.
Already he was fast becoming indispensable. And now he
was getting rid of Jed.

Jed half turned away, but his watery eyes searched Dal's.
Suddenly Allie saw his attention hone in on the shiny ob-
ject hanging around Dal's neck. She peered at it, but all she
saw was what she had before: a small coin tarnished with
age. Nothing exceptional.

"I know you!'' Jed burst out. "I know who you are.''

Dal considered the man before him with narrowed eyes.
"I don't think so.''

"Yeah—I seen you on a ranch east o' here.''

"No.'' Dal's face hardened into implacable lines. He was
furious, Allie realized, not understanding the undercurrents that arced between the two men.

"Dal, what's this all about?'' she demanded, growing
more concerned by the moment. Dal's fist on the gate was
clenched, as was the other, hanging with deceptive casualness by his side, and he looked as if he wanted to smash at
least one of them into Jed's sly face.

"You can say all the things you want about me,'' Jed told
her, his voice almost shrill. "I may be a loafer and a gam-

bler—maybe even a drunk. But I'm not a murderer." He pointed a bent finger straight at Dal's chest. "At least I'm not like him. I never killed a man!"

Chapter Two

"*Murder?*" Allie breathed, turning slowly to face Dal. "Did he say...murder?"

Dal stood statue-still, watching Jed hightail it out to his rusted sedan and roar away. The features of his handsome face were strained, his shoulders stiff. "I'll leave," he said. "I'll be on my way as soon as I can collect my gear."

With that he swung about and strode for the bunkhouse.

He made it halfway there before Allie could uproot herself. "Wait!" She raced after him. After only four days' work, he'd proven to be the best hired hand she'd ever had. He was capable, knowledgeable, kept to himself and worked hard. She couldn't let him just ride off!

She caught at him and noticed that beneath her fingers the muscles of his forearm were taut. "Tell me what Jed meant exactly. I think you should explain."

Politely he shook off her hand and kept walking. "It's best that I leave now."

"No!" She grabbed at his arm again, this time succeeding in turning him toward her. "Just tell me. Did you...kill someone?"

"Yes."

She searched his face, looking for signs of malice, for some terrible hint of a conscienceless killer. But all she saw was the tense, wooden features of a man caught in the grip of inner frustration. His eyes were pale green, she noticed fleetingly, appearing even paler next to his dark lashes. Now, they were narrowed and bright with tension. Allie swallowed and couldn't seem to get her voice above a whisper. "Murder?"

"Not murder...exactly."

"Are you on the lam?"

He looked startled at that. "What?"

She swallowed again. "Are you running from the law?"

"No!" He pivoted away, letting her see only his profile, and his jaw muscles clenched. His hat threw the rest of his face into shadow.

"What happened?"

Facing her again, Dal met her gaze squarely. "No questions. Either you want me here or you don't."

A long silence stretched between them while Allie frantically considered. She had her daughter to think about, and herself. How could she keep a possibly dangerous man around? Should she believe Dal—who refused to explain further—or should she let him go and take no chances?

So far, he'd been a model employee. He had worked as hard as two men and had taken over chores she hadn't even assigned him. He'd appeared promptly at mealtimes, been scrupulously polite to her and kept to himself in the bunkhouse at night. More importantly, he had an aura of honest forthrightness—a directness that forbade subterfuge. How could she let him go when he might very well help keep them all from bankruptcy?

The decision appeared to be a matter of faith.

Breathing deeply, Allie told him, "If you say you're innocent, then I'll have to believe you. I want you to stay. The fact is, I need you." She gestured in the direction in which Jed had made his escape. "You see the kind of hired man that's available to me. The truth is—" she paused, then blurted "—you're a godsend."

Instead of relaxing a bit, as Allie had expected, Dal's features hardened even more until his frown was fierce. "I'm *nobody's* godsend, hear? I can't allow myself to be made responsible for anyone else—I won't be. I'll work for you, boss lady, but only for a time. The minute you start relying on me, I'll be gone." With that he swung around and headed in the direction of the horse corrals, and Allie watched while he whistled up his big gelding.

She hoped against hope she wasn't jeopardizing her safety. But if he was going to do something bad, wouldn't he have already done it? She made her way to the house, deciding a call to the local authorities wouldn't hurt. Passing that test, she told herself, Dal's past wouldn't matter to her in the least. Not as long as he continued to work hard.

An hour later at the ancient oak desk that had once been her father's, Allie slumped, placing her head in her hands. Around her were scattered the general ledgers of the ranching operation—old receipts and invoices. Her father's neat handwriting had grown sloppy and careless in the last year of his life.

Allie felt the familiar wash of guilt envelop her. She should have been here, helping her father care for her cancer-stricken mother. If she'd known, she could have helped run the ranch. Instead, the place had been increasingly neglected until her mother's death, and her father's of a stroke a mere two months later.

But she hadn't been there. She'd been living in San Antonio, waitressing and trying to raise Jessie, afraid to return home after her shameful defection. She'd been afraid of the censure and disappointment in her gentle mother's eyes. For four years, she stayed away.

Without her they'd both sickened and died. She hadn't even known about their illnesses until their estate attorney had tracked her down through her employer.

So now she'd been home for nearly a year. She'd had a whole year to shore up the faltering cattle business her father had loved...but it hadn't happened. Instead, the expertise to put such a business back in the black escaped her and finances were in even worse shape. It seemed imperative that she keep the place—the home of her parents dreams—and keep it well. But how could she?

Outside the small window a movement caught her eye and she rose to look. Dal was piling the truck with feed, working hard. Again she was struck by the strange premonition that he could be her ranch's savior. He could help her as no one else.

Instantly Allie turned away and shook off the fanciful thought. "Don't be ridiculous," she mumbled. Dal was just a man, like any other. Nothing more.

Still, she didn't make the call to the local sheriff. She would, of course, and soon. But not...yet.

Dal hauled hundred-pound sacks of protein feed into the back of the old pickup, then headed for the hay loft. There he piled the truck high with sweet-smelling bales. Winter feeding cattle was a monotonous, back-breaking job, but necessary in times of drought, when forage for the animals was sparse, and during winter months when cold temperatures slowed grass growth. Dal hated it.

He'd much rather be on horseback, whirling his rope overhead in preparation to snag some wayward calf or ornery steer. He liked riding pastures, checking on windmills and fence lines, observing cattle and watching them thrive and fatten. But that was mostly summer work, and now it was just past dead winter. A good month or two of winter feeding still remained in the season.

"Damn," he muttered as a piece of baling wire bit through his too-thin gloves and bruised his hand. He rubbed at it and couldn't imagine the slender Allie lifting and loading heavy bales day in and out. It was this job that had actually convinced him to stay on. He couldn't leave her ranch now, consigning her to the strenuous work that should be reserved for men.

Over by the horse corral he spotted Allie speaking softly to her palomino mare inside. Dal wondered about her past. Where was her husband? Her parents? Didn't she have anyone to support her financially...emotionally? Why was she struggling all alone?

The idea made Dal angry, but quickly he tamped down the feeling. He wasn't here to become involved or make judgments. It was none of his business.

Out in the west pasture, Dal honked the pickup's horn, and the small herd of cows and calves began trotting toward the truck, knowing it carried food. He got into the bed and threw off the feed, counting heads and looking for signs of trouble.

Dal shook his head and wondered how Allie had kept them in such good shape. She was fighting a losing battle, a hopeless situation, and she must know it. It galled him that she'd called him a godsend, and he let out a scoffing laugh.

He couldn't save her sorry excuse of a spread. Sooner or later she'd lose. All he could do was stave off the inevitable.

Dal dumped off the last bale with a shove somewhat harder than necessary. He drove back to ranch headquarters for more hay and noticed a new, sky-blue pickup parked at the front gate. He wondered what sort of idiot painted his pickup sky blue.

The idiot was tall and tanned and lean. He wore tight-fitting blue jeans and his hat sat over his right eye on a jaunty angle that matched the arrogant roll of his gait. He was walking toward Allie with all the direct purpose of a stud bull intent on running down a coy heifer.

Dal knew he should begin loading more cottonseed cake for the east pasture, but he couldn't help wanting to see Allie's reaction to the man. Instead of getting the cake, Dal went first to the barn where he had a clear view of the house and began hefting bales into the truck.

Allie waited for Slade Hunt to come up her front walk, much as she had waited for Dal four days before. But this time with far less hopeful anticipation. *Caution* might be a better word, she decided ruefully. She and the neighboring rancher had known each other all their lives, and she had earned many bruises and hurt feelings at his hands. Slade had been a childhood bully.

He seemed to have outgrown that.

"Allie, honey," Slade called in the good-old-boy drawl he favored. "You're looking prettier than a little red heifer in a flowerbed."

She grimaced. "You've got to be kidding."

He stopped at the gate, doffing his hat. "Can I come in? Maybe you've got some hot coffee for a poor old cowboy?"

"Poor old cowboy?" she repeated, opening the gate. "Your ranch is three times the size of mine. Doing a lot better, too," she added in a muttered aside.

"That may be so, honey, but I've been thinking—a woman like you oughtn't to struggle so. I imagine you'll want to round up early this year. What with the drought and all, I figured to get 'em branded and vaccinated within a month or two."

"That sounds like a good idea." She smiled politely, pointing to a chair on her porch. For some vague reason she didn't want to invite her neighbor into the house. "Have a seat. I'll get coffee." As she went inside, she caught sight of Dal standing in the back of the truck amid bales of hay. His hands were propped on his hips and his chest heaved with the exertion of lifting. But his gaze was centered on her and Slade. She was startled to find her taciturn employee frowning at her so directly. It made her feel as if she'd done something wrong. She shook herself and brought out two mugs of steaming brew. "Go on, Slade."

Sprawled across the porch glider, Slade held out a brown hand for one of the chipped mugs. "I was thinking. You've been working darned hard this past year. A pretty gal like you ought to have a better life."

She blinked, confused. It was the same thing Dal had said to her.

He went on. "Truth is, your land's not worth a fortune—you know that—but I might be willing to take it off your hands."

"No!" she said sharply.

"All right, all right. If you mean to stay, I'll be the first to help you." He backtracked so fast she was thrown off balance. Was he offering for her property because he truly wanted it—or as a favor to her?

"Maybe you'd like some help with the branding?" he asked. "I could send over three or four men next month and help get your cattle worked. No charge."

"You mean it?" Allie felt new hope. She took a seat on a whitewashed rattan chair and clutched her mug. "That would be terrific! I was...well, a little worried about how we'd manage all by ourselves."

Slade studied her features, seeming to enjoy her smile. "You know if you ever need help, I'll be there, Allie."

Something in his manner made an unexpected blush bloom across her cheeks. "Thank you, Slade. I—"

A voice from across the yard caught her attention. "You need me to do anything special while I'm out at the east pasture, Allie?" Dal had piled the truck high and he waited beside it with one fist on his hip.

Allie glanced at Dal, startled. She'd forgotten all about him. "Uh, no. You can go now," she called. Turning back to Slade, she was about to express her gratitude when Dal's voice came again.

"Didn't you say there was a fence post that needs replacing, Allie?" Dal hadn't moved.

She frowned. "Just take one of the posts from the barn and replace it, then." To her neighbor she said, "Slade, you don't know how grateful I—"

"And what about that broken windmill?" Dal walked around the side of the truck and opened the passenger door. "Maybe you'd best come along and show me where it is exactly."

Letting her breath out in an impatient little huff, she set her mug on a small table and rose. She was about to tell Dal to find it himself when Slade got lazily to his feet. "It's all right, Allie, you run along and show your hired man how to do his work. I've got to get back, anyway." With that he dropped a hand on her shoulder and stroked her.

Allie forced herself to remain still beneath the unexpected caress. She wasn't sure how to react. Although they had never become friends, she had learned to get along with him.

Yet the male interest in his eyes now charted new territory. Always a womanizer, Slade had cut a wide swath of broken hearts through the ladies of nearby Lubbock. A fine-looking man with ownership of a successful cattle operation, Slade had no trouble finding new conquests.

Until now he'd never seemed interested in Allie as a woman.

Just as she began to worry, Slade's hand slid off her shoulder and he made his way down her front steps.

"Thanks for offering your men for my roundup, Slade," Allie called after him. "I believe I'll take you up on it."

He grinned and touched his hat. "Just being neighborly." He slammed the door of his truck and roared off down the dirt road that led to his ranch. She choked a little at the dust cloud his careless tires tossed up. Inside the house she lifted a drowsy Jessie into her arms and carried her out front. Dal waited at the passenger side of her truck.

"You know him?" he asked curtly.

As she slid into the truck holding a sleepy Jessie, she flicked him an impatient glance. "Of course. He's my neighbor."

Dal got in the driver's side and headed toward the east pasture. "Do all your neighbors have time to stop by in the middle of the day for coffee and...talk?"

"If they're successful and friendly they do," she returned, keeping her gaze straight ahead.

"So, I suppose Mr. Successful and Friendly understands that by offering you use of his cowboys, you can't return the favor?"

"He knows we can't swap cowboys for branding." She clutched the handhold as the top-heavy truck swayed into a rut. "*You* represent my entire work force—and obviously I can't spare you for a week of branding at his place."

"Obviously. It just makes me wonder why he made the offer. There's no profit involved—no gain for him. Maybe there's some other form of payment he has in mind?"

Allie turned sharply to look at Dal, but he was squinting out the dirty front windshield, carefully navigating the rough country. His face was devoid of accusation. Still, she suspected he was alluding to something she'd rather not consider.

Turning back, she thought a moment. "You're right. I probably should try and repay him."

It was Dal's turn to look sharply at her. "Like how?"

She lifted one slim shoulder. "Oh, I don't know. Maybe supply him with eggs for several months."

Out of the corner of her eye she watched while Dal's shoulders relaxed almost imperceptibly. "That sounds like a good idea," he said.

After several moments of silence, Allie commented, "I thought you needed my direction to the broken windmill? You seem to know exactly where you're going."

Dal slowed the truck. "I know up to this point. But you'll have to guide me from here." He glanced at her with an innocence that seemed foreign to his nature.

"You've been riding the pastures for days—you know the land." Suddenly she grew tired of the deception they both seemed to be playing. Especially when she didn't understand exactly *why*. "Look, I think you should know that Slade Hunt is welcome on my ranch anytime. He and I go back a long way, we grew up together. And now he's offering me a valuable service because he cares about me." She added this last on impulse. For some reason she wanted Dal to think she and Slade were friendlier than they truly were. "You'd best not interfere."

"Interfere?" He snorted. "What you do and who you do it with is your concern, boss lady. It's none of mine. I'm just talking business, that's all. Which way to the windmill?" And with that, the subject was closed.

"How old are you?" Jessie leaned against Dal's knee the next afternoon as he sat on the porch during a soda break. Though the day was chilly, with a good west Texas wind hurrying across the prairie, Dal had been working in only a flannel shirt and leather vest. Digging post holes for a small section of fence along the property front was proving to be tough going. The ground was hard and the rusted post hole digger dull. Dal took another long pull of the cool cola before answering the little girl's question.

He touched her nose with the tip of his finger. "I'm twenty-nine years young."

She grinned at him with childish disbelief. "Naw. You're not young. You're *old*."

"Is that right?" He tugged on her dark braid. "Well, how old are you?"

She puffed out her little chest. "I'm almost five."

"Which means you're four."

"No," she told him with great certainty. "I'm almost five."

"I see." Dal smiled.

"Pretty soon I'll have 'nough pennies to buy my pony. Know how many I have? Sixteen!"

"So many?" He ruffled the top of her head. "Tell you what, little tumblebug, if you keep saving, pretty soon you *will* have enough. In fact, I'm willing to take you on as an employee."

"What's a ploy ee?"

"Somebody who works for money. And if you'll fetch me a soda every time I'm thirsty, I'll pay you. In pennies."

"Pennies!" she cried. "I'll get you a soda right now!" She raced off into the house, her vinyl cowboy boots tapping on the wooden boards.

Dal chuckled, and when she came back, he fished in his dusty jeans pockets and came up with a small handful of pennies. Jessie stared at them excitedly and ran back into the house to deposit them into her piggy bank.

He liked Jessie. The girl was open and loving and sweet. What would it be like, he wondered, to watch her grow to womanhood? That first day of school, her first crush, learning to drive? Dal shook his head. Allie was truly lucky. She'd get to experience all the wonders of life with Jess. But he wouldn't. He'd be long gone, probably working cattle at some other spread down the road—moving on—always moving on.

In his mind an endless number of ranches stretched before him. Along with the empty prospect an unexpected yearning to stay in one spot gnawed at him. Would he ever get more from life than he already had—his hat, his horse and rigging?

Scowling at his dark thoughts, Dal noticed something moving far off. From the long driveway, a dust cloud transformed into an elderly sedan. The car ground to a halt in the gravel in front of Dal, and when the driver turned off the ignition, the engine gave a loud snort, like a disgruntled steer.

"Howdy." The driver called as he got out, and Dal tipped his hat. The boy was about seventeen, tall and lanky. "You the new man?"

"That's right." Dal waited at his post on the porch. In the Old West, a man didn't ask for names. Too many had come from the east to Texas and beyond to start new lives, leaving behind shadowy pasts.

Back then a man could get shot and killed for asking personal questions of nervous drifters. Dal figured it was too good a tradition to throw away, one that suited him. So he didn't ask this young man's name.

"I'm Pete," the kid said, solving the matter. Eagerly the lad came forward, extending a hand. "I help Allie around here after school and on weekends. But I don't...uh, know much. I guess I'll be working for you now, huh?"

Shaking the boy's hand, Dal allowed himself a small grin. "Guess so. I'm Dal, and glad to meet ya. Today's your lucky day, Pete. You're gonna learn to dig post holes."

"Oh." Pete's returning grin was rueful as he stuck his hands into his front pockets. "Sounds like a lot of fun."

Some thirty minutes later, sweaty and dirty, Dal had unbuttoned his shirt and rolled up his sleeves. He drove the post hole digger repeatedly into the unforgiving earth while Pete scooped out dirt with an old coffee can.

Out of the corner of his eye Dal caught sight of Allie using clothespins to hang wet laundry onto a line that was strung from the side of the house out to a high post. Today she wore her habitual blue jeans, so faded by washings and fresh-air dryings that they clung softly to her trim thighs and rounded derriere.

Strapped at her waist was the belt buckle she had a habit of clutching when she was nervous, and Dal wondered about it. It was obviously a trophy buckle, with an etching of a bucking horse done in fine silver and turquoise, but he never got close enough to read the engraving.

Dal gave the digger a few more downward thrusts and drew to a stop, panting. "I think I'll let you have a turn, Pete," he suggested, passing over the tool and bending to take the coffee can.

"But you dig so well—I couldn't do as good a job as you, Dal," the boy said, grinning.

"There's no teacher like experience," Dal returned. He smiled back and took off his hat to wipe sweat from his brow. That's when he noticed the lone rider, standing perfectly still several hundred yards away on top of a nearby knoll.

The rider was watching Allie.

Pete noticed the direction of Dal's attention. His grin faded. "Slade Hunt," he explained.

"The neighboring rancher?"

"You know him?"

"He stopped by yesterday. Offering favors."

Pete scratched his chin, sprouting with new whiskers. "He does that sometimes. Just comes by. But more often he rides to the top of that hill and just watches her."

Both pairs of male eyes went to Allie, still hanging laundry. She bent into her wash basket and drew out two sets of feminine underwear—one tiny and pastel colored—the other woman sized, filmy and pale pink. As she stretched toward the line, her breasts strained against the thin cotton of her button-down shirt.

Dal felt his jaw muscles tighten. "Does she know he's there?"

Pete shrugged. "She never looks up. He's pretty far away—maybe she doesn't see him. Or maybe she does and she's ignoring him. Either way, it appears to mean the same thing."

"Which is?"

Pete shrugged again. "She's not interested. Can't say as I blame her."

"Why not?" Perversely, he wanted to know.

Between digging efforts, Pete said, "Slade likes the ladies. Lots of 'em. Allie's too smart to fall for that."

"Is she?"

"Sure. She knows Slade Hunt is bad business. Say, you gonna scoop out that dirt?"

"Yeah, right." Dal bent to the task, but he was hard-pressed to take his eyes off the man on horseback watching Allie with eerie patience.

Suddenly Dal got the disturbing image of a circling vulture waiting for a weak calf to quit struggling.

He didn't like the other man looking at Allie as if he had a right to. He didn't like the man's manner.

Again he baled dirt and rocks from the hole, his eyes stealing back to Slade Hunt. He had to squelch the urge to throw the man off Allie's land.

Suddenly he was disgusted with himself, angry. Allie Pearson hadn't asked for his help, nor did it appear that she wanted it. This wasn't his place, nor were the people here his concern. He'd do best to keep his mind on his own business. From now on, he would.

Chapter Three

Allie leaned on the end of her shovel and watched Jessie burst into the end stall where she was mucking out. Jess clutched a mewling calico kitten to her chest and along its eye was smeared a clear goo.

"My kitty! My kitty's gonna get all better. See! See the medicine, Mommy?"

Allie inspected the cat "Medicine? Who...?"

In the doorway Pete appeared. "Dal treated the cat," he informed Allie. It was Sunday morning and he'd arrived for work early, wearing faded overalls and a once-navy baseball cap that had seen better days. "Dal said Jessie's kitten had some chaff in its eye," he went on, admiration evident in his open face. "And he found an old tube of ophthalmic ointment in the tack room."

Allie's gaze went from Pete's face to her beaming daughter. "That's fine," she said, giving the kitten's head a little scratch. She grasped the shovel and resumed scooping dirtied straw into a wheelbarrow.

"Dal sure knows a lot," Pete remarked, making Allie pause again. "More than Jed or any of the others we've had around here."

Glancing over her shoulder, Allie wondered at the boy's enthusiasm over Dal. The man had only been on the ranch a week. "Why don't you fill the watering troughs, Pete?"

"Sure, Allie. I was just about to do that." He tugged his cap more securely onto his sandy hair and hurried off.

Allie shook her head and smiled to herself. She finished with the last of the straw and lifted the handles of the heavy wheelbarrow. Outside at the manure pile behind the barn, she dumped it and paused as she noticed Dal dismounting.

He had gathered two yearlings and brought them into the small pen adjacent to the barn. As she watched, Dal took two syringes, a bottle of medicine, a patch cut from old blue jeans and some strong glue out of a bucket he had placed just outside the pen. He filled the first syringe and called for Pete.

Other than a quick nod to Allie, he took no more notice of her. She wondered what he planned to do.

Pete came at a run.

"Can you rope?" Dal asked Pete without preamble.

The ground at Pete's booted feet seemed to have captured his interest. "I'm, uh, learning."

"It's okay," Dal said. "I'll pitch a rope over one of the yearlings, and then hand it to you. Just take a wrap or two around this stout post and hold him while I throw him. Then we can get him doctored."

"Pinkeye?" Pete said, and Allie was chagrined when she realized both calves showed definite signs of the mild eye disorder. She should have spotted the condition right off.

"Right. It's lucky I still carried some antibiotics with cortisone in my saddle bags, or we'd have to go to town." He took down his lariat from his saddle, shook out a loop and snagged the calf on the first try. While Pete held the line taut, Dal approached the calf and threw it onto its side. With a piggin' string he quickly spun three circles around the calf's legs. From nearby he retrieved the syringe, patch of denim and glue.

Allie watched in approval as Dal deftly shot the medicine into the calf's eye, then drew a wide circle of glue around it. Over this he laid the patch. He performed the same procedure with the other calf.

Pete seemed fascinated. "Are we gonna have to catch them and take off that covering when the eye's better?"

"Naw," Dal returned. "It'll fall off in a couple of weeks and the eye'll be good as new."

As they talked, Jessie ran up, her normal headlong speed impeded only slightly by her armload of four kittens. Allie watched as Dal chuckled at the sight, and she couldn't help smiling herself. Jessie said, "Does my kitty need a patch?"

"Your kitty will be just fine with the medicine we gave her," Dal said. He hunkered down and spoke softly to the kittens, and Allie was strangely curious about what he was saying.

She drew closer and leaned against one of the corral rails. With his big fingers he gently inspected each feline eye, murmuring words so low Allie couldn't catch them. Aloud she wondered idly, "You been around animals all your life, Dal?"

He shrugged, the faintest shadow of reserve returning to his manner. Straightening, he began putting away the implements. "I guess."

"Well, you sure are good with eyes," she observed, smiling at him. "If I ever get a problem with one, I'll know who to come to."

He said nothing for a minute, merely studied her, a faint smile hovering around the edges of his hard mouth. "I don't suppose you'll ever have a problem. Your eyes are pretty. The color of a Texas sky in summer."

Allie froze. Dal complimenting her? Somehow he hadn't seemed the poetic type—certainly not one to pass out flattery so easily.

But he didn't appear to think anything amiss. He merely went on with what he was doing.

"Dal," Jessie demanded, "do these other kitties need medicine?"

"No. They're fine." He dropped the syringe into a small container of disinfectant. Suddenly Jessie set down her burden and threw herself around Dal's leg. The cats scattered in all directions.

Dal glanced down, startled.

"Thank you, thank you, thank you!" Jessie crowed, grinning up at the big man as she hugged him.

For a short second Dal appeared completely disconcerted. Then, with a hand that hadn't seemed awkward at all when he'd caressed the kittens, he gave Jessie's back a clumsy pat. He sought Allie's gaze.

Allie couldn't help frowning. Her small pleasure at his compliment a moment ago instantly fled. Getting on her good side was one thing—insinuating himself with her Jessie was another. She had to fight the impulse to run over and yank her daughter away from the taciturn cowboy. She didn't like seeing Jessie offer affection to Dal, whose background was suspect. She didn't like realizing he was, at this moment, deserving of it.

"Jessie," she snapped. "Come in the house. It's lunchtime." Hoping he read the warning in her glance, Allie gestured Jessie close, and when the girl came, Allie held her protectively against her side.

Something flickered in Dal's eyes, but he said nothing, merely mounted his gelding and signaled Pete to open the gate. The yearlings loped out and he followed, turning them back toward the west pasture.

* * *

"I want to replace the fence between our land and Slade's, too, Dal, but since you've seen fit to offer advice about this, you'd better understand that money's tight." Allie settled her bottom more comfortably on the bench seat of the truck as she bounced along between Pete and Dal. Jessie sat quietly on Pete's lap. "I think it's more important to use the small amount of extra money I have for buying replacement heifers come spring."

"Your cows are old, Allie, I'll give you that." Dal guided the pickup toward Lubbock with the same casual ease he sat his horse. "But most have a good year or two of calf producing left in them. What you need now is to string new fencing. Hunt's cattle have no respect for that sorry excuse of a property line."

"But we can patch the fence. Now that I've got those three blooded Charolais bulls, we need better cows. Those bulls are only going to produce as good a calf as the cows can turn out." Allie stared at Dal's stern jaw, and her own chin lifted. She wasn't accustomed to having employees argue with her. Even if they did make some sense. Pete wasn't helping at all, merely sitting quietly at her right with his long thin legs outstretched. And Jessie was uncharacteristically silent on his lap, looking out the window and hugging her doll.

Dal sighed and with a callused thumb nudged his hat onto the back of his head. "I agree with you about the heifers, Allie. And you should buy new ones. But not now when there are more pressing matters. It'll be two years before they can even begin producing for you—meanwhile Hunt's cattle are trampling your old fence and eating what forage is left in the east pasture." He took his attention off the road for a long moment to pin her with his pale eyes. "Furthermore, if Hunt has any bulls running with that herd, and they get to your cows, you're going to see calves dropping all year round." He shook his head. "That's not good ranch management."

Suddenly Allie wearied of the fight. She crossed her arms and stared ahead out the window. "I wonder where you get all your fancy ideas about *ranch management?*" When he refused to answer, her annoyance grew. "Oh, I forgot. I'm not allowed to wonder about you, am I?"

She had the satisfaction of seeing Dal's jaw tighten.

"Besides," she went on, some devil urging her to see if she could truly goad the laconic man, "you're just a working cowboy, aren't you? You really aren't qualified to offer advice on how I or anyone else should run a ranch."

He glanced at her sharply, eyes narrowed, and Allie had the distinct impression he was angry. She'd guessed a big, capable man like him wouldn't like being put in his place. Certainly not by a poor ranch woman like herself. Yet for some reason his irritation didn't give her the pleasure she'd expected.

Dal pulled up to Lubbock Feed Barn and cut the engine. They all got out and Allie went straight up the steps and inside. She walked past rows of new saddlery, bags of animal feed and racks of Western clothing. Two men she knew tipped their hats respectfully and she waved a hello.

Then Allie's steps automatically faltered. Leaning against the counter where she wanted to place her order was Slade Hunt. With one long tanned finger he was stroking the underside of the girl's chin who leaned against the counter from the other side. Teenaged Tricia Anderson, a pretty redhead and the daughter of Lubbock Feed Barn's owner, gazed adoringly up into Slade's grinning face.

But when she spotted Allie her smile vanished.

Slade glanced over his shoulder, and he straightened without a trace of self-consciousness. "Allie, honey, why didn't you tell me you were comin' to town today? I could've picked up whatever you need."

"Thank you for the offer, Slade, but I don't mind coming into town." Coolly, she nodded to the girl behind the counter. "Tricia."

"Hi, Allie." The girl nodded back without enthusiasm.

As Allie read off her list of supplies to Tricia, she tried to ignore Slade's stare. The man's infernal grin never wavered. After years of trying to either show courtesy to him or ignore him, she was almost used to his blatant inspections. Almost.

When she finished with her list, she couldn't stand it anymore. "Did something happen today to put that big smile on your face, Slade?"

He put one finger beneath her chin, much as he'd done to Tricia, and said softly, "A man will always smile at a pretty woman, Allie. And I wouldn't be much of a man if I didn't smile at you."

As she had at the ranch just a few days ago, Allie went still beneath Slade's hand. His fingers slid smoothly up her face to cup her cheek and she found herself staring into his rich brown eyes. Within seconds she discovered that his direct gaze somehow mesmerized her. Slade was rakish and confident—and even his arrogance had a certain sexual appeal. She was powerless to move.

He might as well have shouted *"Let's go to bed!"* for all that she could have missed his message. Yet even through all this she was left cold. It suddenly occurred to her that if somehow Slade could come into ownership of her land, his spread would be the largest in that part of west Texas. She jerked her chin away and glared at him coolly. Paxton's eyes had been that exact shade of brown.

In Paxton's eyes she'd thought she'd read enduring love—where there had only been careless affection. She had thought she'd seen loyalty and strength—where there'd been merely passing whimsy... irresponsibility.

Paxton had left her to raise Jessie alone.

To Slade she said, "You'd best wait for an invitation before you touch me again." She stepped away, gave curt in-
structions to Tricia about her order and strode toward the
door. But she was surprised to catch sight of Dal, where he
stood in front of a wall of new leather bridles. A headstall
with ornate stitching dangled from his fingers, but he was
frowning at her. When their eyes met, he gave her a hard
stare, then turned deliberately away, and his words of a few
days ago rang in her mind. *What you do and who you do it
with is your concern, boss lady. None of mine.*

An inexplicable disappointment settled briefly around
Allie. She impatiently shook it off. Outside, she directed
Pete to start loading the truck while Jessie played with her
doll in the cab. Dal came out a moment later and began
helping. Heading back toward the ranch, no one said anything, and it wasn't until they neared Lubbock's city limits
that she noticed Pete's restless squirming.

"She made a fool of herself!" he burst out. "Am I right,
or did I imagine it?"

Mystified, Allie turned toward him. "Imagine what?"

"You didn't notice Tricia mooning over Slade Hunt?" he
asked.

"It seems," Dal said laconically, "like a lot of women
do."

"Not Allie," Pete shot back. "When he put the moves on
her, she just walked away." He shifted Jessie into Allie's
arms and the girl laid her head sleepily on Allie's shoulder.
Pete stared out his window. "How could Tricia fall for a
jerk like Hunt?"

"Pete," Allie protested, "don't be so hard on her. Slade
is a good-looking man, and he knows how to compliment a
woman—knows what to say to her."

"Does he?" Dal interjected softly.

"I don't care about that," Pete said. "He's too old for her. He's got to be at least thirty." He snorted, as if that age was ancient.

Allie said nothing. Slade *was* too old for Tricia, but he wasn't too old for her. Many might consider their seven-year age difference just right. "He's in his prime," she said, more to herself than to Pete.

Beside her Dal guided the truck to the long stretch of road leading out of town and gunned the accelerator. He had to grit his teeth to keep from giving Allie a lecture about avoiding men like Slade Hunt.

He knew that kind. Men like Hunt needed acquisitions like they needed air. The Slade Hunts of the world didn't give, they just took. They went after women with a covetous greed that flattered and charmed the wary as well as the unwary. And Slade was greedy for Allie.

At the ranch Dal pulled up to the barn and let Pete out to feed the horses. When Allie made to get out, too, he put a staying hand on her arm. "Pete and I can unload. You need to take Jessie and get dinner started, don't you? I'll give you a ride up to the house."

Dal was annoyed by the surprise in her eyes. Hadn't anyone ever shown her chivalry? Hadn't a man ever taken over the tough jobs? "Well," she said slowly, "if you're sure you don't need me."

"I think Pete and I can handle it," he replied dryly. She slid back in and he coasted the truck to the house. Once there, he cut the engine, and as she started to get out, he twisted toward her and again touched her arm. "You hung out laundry last Friday."

"That's right." She eyed him curiously.

"You make a habit of hanging out your underthings for every passing rancher to see?"

She gasped at the unexpected attack. "I can't help it if someone happens by and notices. I don't have a clothes dryer."

"So you did see Hunt."

She shrugged. "I do wash every Friday. I guess he knows it."

"Then why do you ignore him?"

"I don't! It's just ... he doesn't always come up to the house, so I go about my business. He doesn't appear to want anything."

"You don't think so?" Dal asked softly. Lifting her long braid, he rubbed the soft strands between his fingers. They felt as soft as corn silk. Gentle scents rose up—not purchased scents—but natural smells of crushed herbs, like thyme and sage. He inhaled deeply. "I think he wants something."

"No." Allie hugged her sleeping daughter a little tighter. "He's just my neighbor."

"I see." Dal played with the ends of her braid, and she watched his fingers as if fascinated by them. When she swallowed and her hand slid beneath Jessie to touch her silver buckle, he eyed the movement. "Nervous?"

"Of course not. Why would I be?" For the first time she faced him across the seat, and her frown was fierce. "I assume you value your job. You wouldn't ... uh, do anything."

"No?" His hand slid up her braid to her nape. Her skin was warm, probably even warmer than it should be. Was she affected by him? In a gentle whisper he asked, "Do you want to?"

"What?"

"Do something?"

She swallowed again and Dal felt himself drawn far stronger to her vulnerability than he'd ever been to feminine wiles. For once he wished Jessie weren't with them.

Allie was mere inches away, inches from being held against his chest. Already, images of how her breasts would feel against him were flooding his mind. He pictured her nipples responding, tightening, and his body reacted accordingly.

To distract himself, Dal forced his gaze to out the front window. He enjoyed just talking with Allie. She intrigued him, always held his interest. Beside him he heard Jessie sigh in her sleep. "You're a good mother, Allie."

"Thank you." She studied her broken nails.

"Do you think you'd ever like more kids?"

Instantly her eyes flew to his. "I don't see how. But I love Jess." She lifted a hand to caress the girl's hair. "She's my life. Jessie and this ranch."

"But if you marry—"

"I won't. I haven't time for a husband." Surprising him, she grinned. "Or the energy. Husbands expect love and attention and time."

"And right now your ranch gets all your love and attention and time?"

"And Jess."

He inclined his head. "She deserves it. She's a peach."

"How about you? Think you'll ever want children?"

Eyes narrowing, Dal considered a tall, slim boy, growing in his image, and a petite, feminine girl he could call his own. A slow yearning welled in his gut. How could he have children without a wife? And how could he have a wife without a home—respectability—stability—as a good woman deserved?

"I move around a lot," he said tightly. "I don't suppose most women would stand for that."

"No, I don't suppose they would."

"You wouldn't, would you, Allie?" he asked almost diffidently. His hand slid down her braid again.

Something hardened in her eyes. "Not a chance. If I ever *do* decide to marry, it'll be to a steady, reliable man. Someone who'd be content to work all his life right here, because this is where I'll be."

"It must be nice to know exactly how your life will run, where you'll live, what you'll do."

"Nice?" Her forehead wrinkled. "I guess it's better than drifting." Wincing at her own words, she put a hand on his chest. "Sorry. I didn't mean to criticize you."

He smiled, responding more to the feel of her small palm over his heart than to her words. "It's okay. A pretty woman can get away with a lot. And you're as pretty as a spring flower, Allie," he told her. "And smart, too. But you know what I like about you best?"

One fair brow arched. "At the moment you seem intrigued with my hair."

He chuckled. "No. It's the fact that you're one ornery woman."

Her mouth curved up. "Flattery will get you anywhere with an ornery woman." Her eyes skittered away almost shyly. "I think I'd better go in now."

"Stay, Allie. Just another minute." He let his gaze drop to her mouth and made his intentions clear.

"I think," she said, backing away an inch, "that another minute would be too long."

When she slipped out of his grasp and the truck to carry her daughter up the steps of the house, he didn't protest. With morose eyes he watched her disappear and hauled in a deep, hurtful breath. She was right, of course, to escape him. He could never do anything to deserve a warm, sweet woman like Allie.

Swearing bitterly, he twisted the ignition and threw the truck into reverse. At the barn, he slammed the door, placed his palms on the open tailgate and hung his head between his shoulders. He'd had a home once. A family who'd welcomed him. But in one moment of urgency he'd forever altered the course of the life he'd always taken for granted. To have taken a man's life went against everything he'd known.

For two years now he'd been a drifter, moving from ranch to ranch and never staying long enough to develop ties or become irreplaceable. Here was a place he could easily grow attached to. The land was good, producing country. The life-style suited him. And Allie . . . she suited him more than any woman he'd ever dreamed about.

But inside him so much was dead. He couldn't change the past—couldn't rectify it. He wasn't worthy of Allie's love. He would continue the wandering life.

In truth Slade Hunt was more deserving of Allie than he was. Dal swore again and vowed that if Allie wanted Hunt, he wouldn't distract her. Or stand in Hunt's way.

Inside, Allie tried not to analyze her reaction to Dal and set about boiling pasta for the spaghetti sauce she'd been simmering in a crock pot all day. Jessie had awakened and played on the floor with child-sized pots and pans.

Why had she reacted so strongly to Dal's obvious innuendo? She should have brushed off his comments about "doing something" with him as a typical male pass, as she'd done with other men.

But she hadn't. Even with Jessie held between them in the truck's cab, Allie had felt deliciously weak as he'd toyed with her braid and his eyes had taken on that light of interest and heat. He'd looked as if he'd wanted to kiss her. Dear Lord, but she'd *wanted* him to kiss her.

But he was a killer!

Allie grabbed forks from the drawer and slammed it shut with her hip a good deal harder than necessary. Striding to the table, she slapped them down, then went back to hunt for clean place mats. Would she never learn about men!

Dal and Pete came in, washed up and waited for her to serve. After getting Jessie settled at the table, Allie carelessly pushed two heaping plates of spaghetti and French bread in front of the men. A bit of pasta slid off Dal's plate, and he looked up with a questioning eye. She frowned at him, then stepped back to get the salad.

Placing the bowl in the center of the table, she helped herself and Jessie, ignoring the men. Since normally she'd have served them, too, she knew they noticed. The two exchanged perplexed glances, which inexplicably angered her even more.

"It's good, Allie," Dal offered after trying a bite. "The best sauce I've ever tasted."

"Yeah," Pete added, mouth full. "Real good."

Allie eyed them balefully. "Thanks."

Dal's strong teeth sank into a slice of bread and he addressed Pete. "Tomorrow I'll need your help getting those horses in. It's time we started getting them broke to work again. If Allie's cows are ever gonna get marked, I'll need at least seven to nine good working horses."

"Sure, Dal," Pete said. "But why so many? Your big gelding looks strong enough."

Dal chuckled, pleased. "Black Jack's descended from Three Bars. Raised him myself."

"Three Bars? Wow." Pete was impressed enough to stop eating for a moment. "The original quarter horse stallion."

"Yep. But even Black Jack can't work all day every day. Horses'll run out of steam after enough work. I'll need a good string I can rely on."

Allie said nothing because she knew he was right. She adjusted Jessie's cotton-quilted bib. Part of her liked hearing Dal talk about the ranch, but she fought that feeling. He had said not to get dependent on him, and she had to listen—to that, not her own foolish longings.

She should have called the local sheriff long ago. At least to inquire if Dal might truly be wanted by the law. It was unforgivable—*stupid*—of her not to have made one simple phone call. She didn't look up even when she knew Dal's eyes were on her.

"Did you know," he asked her, "about the new crop of foals your horses have?"

"Of course I do," she snapped. "I've ridden out several times to check on them. Don't you think I know what's going on, on my own ranch?"

When he said nothing at all, she felt her anger deepen. There was no further conversation until after dinner.

Dal helped not at all after the meal by starting into a game of gin rummy with Pete, then by making an ostensibly offhanded remark about Jessie's father.

"I guess she favors him," Dal concluded, eyes going over the little girl's dark head. "Because she doesn't look so much like you, Allie."

Instantly most of her anger fled and uneasiness took its place. "I guess," she replied, gaze slipping to read Pete's expression. Was he too young to remember the small scandal she'd caused five years ago by running off with the motorcycle-riding Paxton?

Other than showing mild curiosity, Pete looked completely ignorant of the situation, and Allie relaxed a bit. There was no reason on earth Dal should know of her ignominious past. None but a desire to keep intact his good impression of her. It was a small thing, really, she chastised herself. So what, if one of the ranch hands found out the truth of her sordid past? Still, she quickly changed the subject.

And she would telephone the sheriff. Soon. Just as soon as she got some spare time.

Within a few minutes Pete excused himself to head home. Jessie went to bed, leaving Allie alone with the big cowboy.

She'd been comfortably alone in the house before with men, hands who'd worked the ranch, local cowboys. But Dal was different. He made her edgy, uneasy, self-conscious. She wondered why.

Perhaps it was his quiet ways. He never offered information about himself. If she could get him talking about his life, maybe he'd seem less mysterious and she'd be able to relax around him. Then the faintly volatile air of unpredictability that surrounded him would dissipate.

"Will you clear?" she asked, moving to the sink. "I'll wash."

He said nothing, merely rose from where he'd been sitting at the table and began carrying plates to her.

Soap suds and steaming water filled the sink. She began washing and stacking the cleaned plates in the drainer. "It's a dark night," she commented. "And cold."

He grunted agreement.

"I bet you'd hate to be out riding the range on a night like this."

"Sure would."

"But you put in long days. You get up early and work till dark."

He set the last plate at her elbow. He lifted one big shoulder. "It's a cowboy's life."

"I know." She bit her lip and ventured, "Have you always been a cowboy?"

"In some form or another." Turning his back to the countertop, he leaned against it and crossed his legs at the ankles. In his eyes something flickered. Humor? Anger? She couldn't tell.

His reticence called for a new angle. "I like your hat." She nodded toward the hat rack where it hung. "I guess you paid a bundle for it, huh? Where'd you get it?"

"East Texas."

"That where you're from?" She held her breath.

The light flashed in his eyes again. She rinsed soap off a dish and glanced at him from beneath her lashes. He crossed his arms, the action raising his heavy biceps against his chest. She could see their outlines through his shirt. Tearing her eyes away, she swallowed.

"You want to talk?" Dal asked softly. "All right. We'll talk about you."

"Me?" This wasn't what she had in mind.

"You've had a hard life here. All work and no play. You don't even have your husband to help. He's ... uh ... dead, you said?"

She nodded tightly, squeezed out the sponge and began wiping the counter. If this conversation was going where she thought it was, she could be just as unforthcoming as he!

"Your ... husband—was he a cowboy?"

"No," she answered, and without thinking, told the truth. "Not a cowboy."

"Ah. A businessman?"

A vision of the shiftless Paxton flew before her eyes. "No."

"What then?"

When she made no reply, he touched her shoulder, his face frankly curious. "A lawyer? A construction worker? A mechanic?"

"A mechanic." She seized on the suggestion. Paxton *had* loved to tinker with his motorcycle. Finishing the cleaning, she drew a breath and turned toward Dal, his warm palm still on her shoulder. "Listen, I don't care to talk about—"

"Was he good to you, Allie? Did he work hard for you—treat you with respect? Did he deserve you?"

All at once Allie felt overwhelmed. She blinked, searching Dal's face, looking for traces of sarcasm and finding only genuine concern. *This* cowboy would be such a man. He'd respect his woman, work for her, deserve her. She was certain of it.

He'd taken her other arm now, anchoring her before him. She stood stock-still, unable to move. His hold was almost like an embrace.

Unable to meet his gaze any longer, Allie stared at his shirtfront. Her breathing came shallow and her heart rate escalated. He was so big and tall her head barely met his chin. And he smelled manly in a clean, fresh way she couldn't describe. He was so different from her that next to him she felt tiny and womanly...deliciously weak and feminine. For a split second she imagined kissing Dal. The mental picture of being crushed in his arms and the almost tangible feel of his lips on hers flooded her mind.

Swiftly she turned away, breaking his hold. "I don't like to think about the past. What's done is done, one just has to go on." With stiff movements, she hung two dish towels and cursed her unruly imagination. It was unconscionable—thinking of kissing this—this admitted killer.

From somewhere deep inside, a terrible fear rose up. Fear of losing control. Fear not of what Dal might do—but of what she might allow herself *because* of Dal.

"Yes," he was saying. Still at his post by the sink, his attention was no longer on her. Somehow he'd changed. He looked different, his arms hung loosely at his sides. Even his shoulders had slumped a little, as if in defeat. Almost to himself he said, "You're right. What's in the past can't be changed. Nothing we can do will change it. It's the accepting that's hard."

Quietly she agreed. "I'm tired tonight, Dal. If you don't mind, I think I'll turn in."

"Yes, ma'am." Absently moving by her, he collected his hat and jacket from the hall tree. "'Night."

"Good night." She watched him go, relieved and disappointed at the same time. She'd learned no more about him, excepting her surprising reaction to his touch. Unfortunately, she'd liked it, enjoyed the feel of his masculine hands resting heavily and possessively on her.

In a crazy, wild way it had felt right. But how could it? She'd had her fill of bad men, men without scruples and integrity. Now she wanted to be left alone, or at least exposed only to *good* men.

There was no way of knowing whether Dal was indeed good. Evidence damned him, while her instincts would give him the benefit of the doubt. There would be no way of knowing, she told herself, except by the passing of days and months.

"Time will tell," she whispered, turning off the lamp. "Time will tell."

Disaster struck in the form of an unexpected thunderstorm. The rain turned the hard-packed dirt of the ranch into a quagmire of mud, but did little to alleviate drought conditions. However, it managed to leak through the old barn's roof and wet the precious store of hay.

Unfortunately, it was several days before the damage was noticed, and by then a good portion had gone moldy and rotten. Moldy hay could kill livestock, and Allie couldn't take a chance with the animals. She'd have to buy more.

As she inspected the damage with Dal, she sighed long and hard and suddenly found herself fighting tears. Quickly she turned away and kicked at a bundle of the worthless stuff. She took a surreptitious sniff and wiped her nose.

"Allie?" Dal wielded a pitchfork through a loose flake. She didn't turn. "What?"

"I think we can salvage some of this."

"Yeah. Sure. Maybe twenty percent."

"Or thirty."

"Swell." Allie firmed her lips and climbed the ladder into the loft. She surveyed the silver-dollar-sized holes in the roof. Why hadn't she noticed before? They could easily have been patched and the valuable hay saved.

She took another uneven breath and guessed that with the dry winter, it hadn't occurred to her to watch for possible rain damage.

It was time to face facts.

She could purchase new hay, of course, but the best prices were available in the summer, when hay was harvested. Winter's end was absolutely the wrong time to buy. With her savings account nearly depleted, she wouldn't be able to get the replacement heifers she had her heart set on. Nor could she even consider replacing the fence that Dal had recommended.

Allie knelt to lift a hank of soggy timothy and forced herself to admit that unless she did something drastic, this would be her last year of owning the ranch. Even with Dal's great help, they might well go under.

She stared out the big loft window toward the neighbor's sprawling lands with a gaze that was steady and resigned. It was time to consider other options—including surrendering her land to Slade Hunt.

Chapter Four

Sunday afternoon was a perfect time for catching up on neglected chores, so Allie collected a hammer and nails and crouched over the loose porch board. She really hated this kind of work, but somebody had to do it. Sighing, she prepared to drive in the two-inch nail. As she drew the hammer back, Jessie's furious squeal and an indignant squawking brought her head around. Jessie was chasing a terrified hen across the front yard, the hen flapping her wings and protesting all the way.

Allie lowered the hammer and sat on her heels. "Jess," she called out, "what *are* you doing? Don't you know old Gertie won't lay for days after you scare the dickens out of her?"

Jessie paused in her headlong pursuit to swipe at her bangs. "She's got my necklace! I'm gonna get it back."

"She's *what?*" Sure enough, around the Rhode Island Red's neck something glinted. With the hen darting about the yard at breakneck speed and the four-year-old hard on her tail feathers, Allie had difficulty telling exactly what.

At last Jessie stopped to catch a breath, and the hen slowed. Allie stood, leaned over the porch rail and recognized the plastic string of pink hearts she'd bought for Jessie's Christmas stocking bobbing around the flustered chicken's neck.

From the double barn doors a masculine chuckle rang out.

Dal was leading his black gelding toward the front corral, but he came to a stop and grinned at the scene. "It looks right pretty on that hen, Jessie."

"But it's mine!" the girl complained. "I didn't want her to *keep* it." She glared at the culprit, who strutted in a circle near five or six other hens while keeping a suspicious eye on her persecutor.

"You know, Allie," Dal drawled. "That chicken looks real proud. Notice how she's showing off in front of the others? Maybe you should hang necklaces on 'em all and they'll be so happy they'll lay a couple of eggs a day." He raised an eyebrow at Pete beside him.

"A couple of eggs a day!" Allie had to purse her lips to fight a smile. "Whoever heard of that?" To Jessie this was serious business, and showing amusement would surely hurt her feelings. "Uh, Jess, honey? Let's give old Gertie a chance to calm down, okay? Later we can walk up to her slow and slip it off."

"I want it now." Mutinous anger formed a small frown between Jessie's eyes.

"I'll get it for you," Pete offered, a wide grin splitting his face. He approached the nervous hen with comical stealth, herding her into the small coop. At last he snagged one of her legs and quickly folded her body into his arms. Jessie came at a run. As she was slipping the precious jewelry off, the hen pecked her.

Jessie shrieked and her voice rose in a wail. A minuscule bit of blood appeared on the back of her hand. Oddly, Dal made it to her faster than Allie. He squatted beside her, resting one knee on the hard ground.

"Let me see, little one," he crooned in the same soothing voice Allie had heard him use with the animals. In his big calloused hand Jessie's tiny palm looked fragile as a sparrow's wing. Allie felt a moment's misgiving, but with Pete on her daughter's one side and Dal crowding the other, she couldn't get as close as she liked.

Pressing in, she leaned a hand on Dal's shoulder and peered over to smile reassuringly at the child.

From his neck Dal unknotted a red handkerchief and tied it with great solemnity around the girl's wrist. "This is to protect the wound," he announced very seriously. "We can't be too careful with hen pecks, you know."

Jessie nodded, scrubbing at her tears with the back of her other hand. She held her wounded appendage to her chest. On the ground the pink necklace lay in the dirt. Dal scooped it up and wiped it clean on his jeans, then placed it over Jessie's head.

Like sunshine breaking free of dark clouds, Jessie's sweet smile lit her face. She hiccupped, sniffed and amazingly, giggled. "Thanks, Dal. You're good."

You're good. The words rang in Allie's ears, where she puzzled over them. Why they sounded odd she couldn't imagine. To a four-year-old whose world was made right, it made perfect sense to compliment her savior.

From his squatting position, Dal glanced up at Allie, his face cautiously shaded beneath his hat. He was looking for her reaction, she realized suddenly. He wanted her approval.

She was still leaning against his shoulder. Allie blinked. His back was warm, sturdy. He hadn't protested her weight, had merely borne it without comment or apparent notice. He'd let her lean on him.

Slowly she drew away and cleared her throat. She felt a deep need to hide her feelings and tried to keep her face expressionless. "Uh, it's a good bandage, Dal. We'll just go in and wash up. Thanks."

Murmuring to Jessie, she led the girl up the steps. But at the door she paused and glanced back. Pete had disappeared into the barn, but Dal had merely risen to stand watching her retreat. For the life of her she couldn't identify her own emotions.

Several minutes later she came back out. The porch board had been securely nailed and the tools put away.

It was near dark when Allie realized she had forgotten to get her mail the day before. Pete had stayed on to eat Sunday dinner with them, saying his mother was visiting a friend. He offered to fetch the mail.

"No, thanks," she said, shrugging into her father's denim coat and opening the front door. "I don't mind walking out to the road. But you can clear the dinner dishes for me." She smiled, waiting for Pete's inevitable grimace.

"Aw, I'd rather get the mail," he muttered, but he got up and began stacking dishes.

Beside him Dal grinned. "If you stay gone long enough, Allie, I'll wager old Pete here will have enough time to wash 'em and put 'em all away."

Pete socked Dal's shoulder.

Allie opened the door. "It does take an *awful* long time to walk a hundred yards and back." Chuckling, she let herself into the chilly evening and huddled her chin deep into the coat. She set a quick stride in order to keep warm.

Cicadas buzzed in a small cottonwood close to the mailbox, and Allie smiled at the sound. Her ranch was a peaceful place. Homey and comfortable and safe. She loved it here. Humming low, she opened the trap door and withdrew two envelopes—both advertisements. She sighed.

"No good news?" Slade materialized on horseback in the encroaching darkness less than thirty feet away.

Allie gasped and put a hand to her heart. "You—you startled me."

"Sorry." He nudged his horse closer until he was beside her, staring down. "You don't appear to like your mail. Maybe you were expecting a rich uncle to die and leave you his millions?"

Allie felt a nervous smile curve her mouth. "I don't have a rich uncle. But if I did, he'd probably be a penny-pincher and want to be buried with all his wealth."

Slade laughed. As the sound died away, his smile faded into an intense inspection of her face. "Maybe what you need is somebody to help you along a little, huh?" When she frowned, he said, "No? Then maybe you'll settle for spending time with me. A bunch of us are going to town for dinner tomorrow. You know—Bill and Katie Myers—Dana and her new boyfriend and some others. How about it, Allie," he tossed out carelessly. "Dinner?"

Conflicting emotions raced through her breast—memories of how as a boy he'd torn wings off butterflies and punched her in the stomach until she'd cried. But she also thought about how kind he'd been to her recently—offering use of his cowboys come branding—stopping by for coffee in a neighborly manner.

She thought of her lonely life and of never getting out. Even though she didn't trust Slade, she figured there'd be others she knew close by. An evening in town might be good for her. "Yes, Slade," she answered before any more thoughts could intrude to confuse her. "I'd like to go out with friends."

His spreading grin was so triumphant she almost felt as if she'd agreed to go to bed with him. She put a hand out as if to take it back. "I, uh...just dinner, you understand."

"Sure, sure, Allie. Tomorrow night. Be ready at seven." Reining away, he jabbed sharp-roweled spurs into his horse's flanks and took off at a lazy canter.

From the direction of the house, Allie heard the noises of Pete and Dal coming outside. With solemn faces they watched the rancher ride off then shook hands, and Pete opened the door of his sedan. When Allie got near enough, she heard Pete mutter to Dal, "I'd like to buy him for what he's worth, and sell him for what he *thinks* he's worth."

"Pete!" Allie said sharply and sent him a fierce frown.

He cleared his throat guiltily, thanked her for the meal and promised to come over the next day after school.

Dal waved him off and faced her, but he didn't meet her eyes. Somehow she had the impression he wanted to say something. She waited, her foot resting on the porch board he'd repaired.

Thrusting his hands deep into his front pockets, he turned his head toward the direction in which Slade had ridden off and his jaw tightened. "Nice night for a ride."

"I guess." She eyed him curiously. "I'm not one for riding near dark. I'd rather be inside with my feet up toward a fire."

Dal nodded. "Yeah. Seems that Hunt likes night rides. I see him around here a lot at dusk."

She lifted one shoulder beneath the heavy coat and made an attempt at lightness. "At least I'm not hanging my underwear tonight."

Instead of producing a smile, Dal's face hardened. He opened his mouth, then closed it and grimaced. He looked tense, edgy. "Guess I'll turn in. Thanks for dinner." Face grim, he struck out for the bunkhouse.

"Dal?" she called softly.

He barely glanced over his shoulder. "Yeah?"

"Thank you for fixing the porch." She tested her weight on the board and couldn't make it move. "You did a nice job."

He waved a hand. "It's nothing."

"I forgot something." She dug into her jeans pocket and pulled out a check folded in half. "Here's your pay for the last two weeks."

She thrust it toward him, but he made no immediate move to take it. For a long moment he merely looked at the paper in her hand.

Finally he covered the few steps between them, took the check and stuffed it into his back pocket without looking at the amount.

"It's all there," she told him.

"I know. You wouldn't cheat anybody."

She gazed up at him, trying to read his expression in the dim light. But beneath his ever-present hat she could see little beyond the darkened shadow of the days' beard on his cheeks and the glint of his pale eyes.

He'd gone from avoiding her gaze to a steady stare that was beginning to unnerve her. He put his booted foot beside hers on the repaired board and tested it. "I guess I did do a good job. No squeaks."

Automatically her gaze dropped to their two feet, side-by-intimate-side on the narrow stair. The proximity of his big boot half an inch from her small one made her think of other ways to become close...other intimacies. Suddenly she could smell him. Scents of the soap she kept in the bathroom and he'd used to wash up mingled with faint odors of horse and leather and something that was uniquely Dal.

And she could feel him. He seemed closer than was prudent, and his body warmth radiated to her. Even his gaze somehow joined them with bonds of brooding mental connection. He made her feel restless, uncertain, confused and somehow...excited.

All at once she knew he was thinking of bedding her.

Abruptly he wheeled away, heading for the bunkhouse.

"'Night," she called after him, relief and a conflicting emotion she would never label *disappointment* settled over her. He didn't answer.

The next evening she made herself pretty for her date with Slade.

Jessie bounced on Allie's bed, her butter-yellow blanket sleeper decorated with teddy bears zipped tightly up to her neck. "I like that dress, Mommy. I like blue."

"Thanks, sweetie," Allie returned absently. She brushed her long hair and let it fall to her hips. At her forehead, she used a curling iron to feather a few wispy bangs. Inspecting herself critically in the mirror, she supposed she looked as good as she possibly could in the inexpensive polyester dress and low-heeled shoes. The doorbell rang and she gathered up her purse. She'd arranged for Katie Myers to pick her up. It must be her.

"Wait, Mommy! You forgot makeup." Jessie held out a small case of shadows and blushes.

"I don't want any makeup, Jess."

"You're going out! You gotta have makeup." Jessie rummaged in the case and dug out a plastic lipstick container. "Put some on me first, please?"

Smiling, Allie knelt beside her daughter. "Okay, I guess you're right." With a few strokes, she applied the coral shade to Jessie's rosebud mouth and then to her own. Turning the light low, she lifted the girl onto the pillow and said, "You can stay in my bed until I get home, okay? But you have to close your eyes and go right to sleep. You know Mrs. Thomas doesn't like putting you back to bed."

"I don't like Mrs. Thomas."

"Well, she likes you."

"She smells like old flowers."

Allie chuckled. "It's very nice of her to come over and baby-sit you. So be a good girl for her, okay?"

The girl pursed her lips mutinously, then relented. "Okay."

In the living room Allie found Dal had opened the door. Slade stood on the stoop, his hat in his hands, wearing a smart bolo tie and dress jeans. "Run and get Allie for me, will you?" Slade was saying to the larger man.

Dal made no move, effectively barring the door. "What do you want?"

"I want—there you are, honey." Slade squeezed by Dal and took her arm. "And you look real pretty. I don't believe I've ever seen your hair down before—it's always in that braid." He led her out. "Our evening's all planned. I'm gonna show you a real good time."

Allie nodded, surprised at seeing him. "Uh, Dal? Mrs. Thomas should be here any minute. Do you mind staying with Jessie until she gets here?"

"I don't mind."

She peered past Slade. "Where's the Myerses?"

"I told 'em I'd get you. No sense in them driving all the way here when I'm right next door."

"But they only live four miles away," she protested weakly. She didn't know if she was prepared to be alone with Slade.

"It's no trouble, honey."

Over Slade's shoulder she caught Dal's frown. He said, "Another favor, Hunt?"

Slade grinned. "I don't mind doing favors for Allie. She's worth it." With that he guided her out the door.

Dal remained silhouetted in the open doorway as Slade handed her into the passenger side of his truck and even as he backed out and roared past the mailbox.

Allie pasted a determined smile on her face and turned toward Slade.

The evening turned out more enjoyable than Allie had expected; even Slade was on his best behavior.

At the elegant steak house in town they danced, and Slade held her too close, of course, but Allie tried not to mind. For most of the evening, he'd been an excellent companion, treated her in a gentlemanly manner, entertaining her and the Myerses with wild cow tales.

It wasn't until the long ride home that Slade truly surprised her. He told her he was lonely.

Allie digested this. She found it hard to believe that inside the man she'd always disliked had hidden a frightened, lonely soul. She knew about his harsh upbringing. "I—I guess it was tough for you after Curtis died."

Squinting into the night, Slade said, "Curtis was my best friend as well as my brother." He turned to her and his eyes were hard. "They didn't care about that. When that tractor rolled over him, it was as if their whole world had died. They didn't seem to notice, or care, that I was still alive."

She knew he referred to his parents. "They punished you a lot," Allie said, "those years afterward. I remember your bruises."

The hardness in his expression faded to a sadness that touched her. "I guess troublemaking was the only way to get their attention." Glancing at her, he said, "They're both gone now. I can live my life the way I want. I know I've been bad, Allie," he told her softly. "But I never had anybody good in my life to rub off on me. Nobody good like you."

Allie's eyes widened. "B-but what about all those women I see you with? You always have a girlfriend or a date."

He shrugged, dismissing them.

In the darkened cab Allie stared down at her hands and disliked the uncertainty racing through her. She was a centered person—a woman who had no illusions about who she was and what she wanted from life.

Yet Slade was making her question many of the conclusions she'd always drawn about him. Could he truly be a misunderstood, lonely man? Someone who merely needed the love and compassion of a *good* woman to realize his potential as a giving human being?

As they neared her ranch, the silence between them drew out. It wasn't an uncomfortable quiet, but an introspective one. The faint low-wattage bulb of her porch lamp guided them toward the house, and Slade pulled to a stop outside the gate.

"So, what about it, Allie?" he asked quietly.

"What about what?" She unbuckled her seat belt and pulled her purse into her lap.

"Will you help me? Will you?" He reached out to take her hand and stroke her fingers tenderly.

"I...don't know exactly what you mean, Slade," she said evasively, loath to promise anything while she was uncertain. Her other hand crept around the door handle.

"If I had you, I could do anything—be anything. Wait, don't leave yet."

"I have to go in, Slade." She pulled slowly away and opened the door.

"Think about it, honey," he said, ducking his head to maintain eye contact as she got out.

Tentatively she nodded. He smiled and reached across to close the door. Through the glass he kept smiling as he put the truck into reverse and eased down her driveway. For long minutes she stood in the cold, staring out into the dark where he'd disappeared.

With a sigh she shivered and turned to climb the porch steps. At the top a movement in a dark corner of the porch caught her eye and she gasped. Dal waited in the shadows.

He unfolded from the glider and approached her, shoving his hands into his back jeans pockets. His tan sheepskin jacket hung open but his collar was turned up. His hat was pulled so low over his eyes she couldn't read his expression. "Have a nice time?"

She picked at the catch of her purse. "Sure. Slade's an interesting man."

"What did you do?"

She looked off into the night, remembering their strange conversation. "Had a steak and potato dinner."

"Anything else?" His voice was tight and controlled, and for the first time Allie realized he appeared oddly tense. He stood stiffly unmoving.

"What do you want to know, Dal?" she asked softly, intuitively guessing something was brewing inside him.

"I sure as hell don't want to hear about what you ate for dinner."

"Then what?"

He spun away and took four steps to the rail. He leaned his hands on the wood two-by-eight. "Nothing. I let Mrs. Thomas go earlier. Pete and I brought in a good bunch of geldings today. After looking them over, I'd guess that some of them will make fine cutting horses. I won't really know until I start working with them, though. But they're fat and sassy. Healthy."

She nodded, wondering why he felt the need to tell her this at midnight. "Good."

Pivoting toward her, he asked, "Did you ask Hunt if he's got sick cows? I wanted you to see if any of his cattle are showing swollen hocks or going off feed." He turned away. "Or were you too *busy?*"

Allie ignored his comment. "Why all this concern over that one cow?"

He answered bluntly. "It might be anaplasmosis."

Exhaling painfully, Allie sank onto a chair. "No," she breathed, aghast. It was bad news at a bad time. "We've got to call the vet."

Dal said nothing.

Costly veterinary fees and medications suddenly mounted in her mind and Allie felt panic. "It'll be so expensive. Good Lord, I don't know what to—"

"We won't need the vet," Dal told her gruffly. "At least not past the first visit or so. I know what to do."

Ready to grab any suggestion at all, she got up and quickly closed the gap between them to touch his arm. "What can we do?"

He glanced down at her hand. "Maybe I'm wrong. Only a laboratory examination of the blood will confirm it. That's why you need to talk to Hunt about his cattle. He may have a carrier."

She took a difficult breath and forced out the necessary question. "It if is anaplasmosis—what's the treatment?"

"Intravenous oxytetracycline. Then more fed to the cattle for sixty days will eliminate the carrier state. But you'll have to pay for a lab test first. I think we can keep the costs down after that."

Her outward calm belying her inner fear, Allie said, "Do you suppose Slade has got a carrier?"

"I don't know. Could be. Ticks are typical carriers, too— also wild animals like deer—or it could be contracted by poor sanitary procedures during castration and vaccination."

"It could be anything!" Allie felt like crying. Her fingers sank into his arm—she needed his strength right now. "But at least you know how to treat it." A new thought distracted her. "How *do* you know so much?"

"I've been around." His eyes seemed fixed on her hand, still resting along the rough fabric of his jacket. "Meantime, you have to let me patch those broken sections along Hunt's fence. I've had to turn back two bunches of steers with his brand. If it turns out his cattle are infected, I want to keep your herds apart."

"Yes, Dal," she agreed immediately. "I suppose I'm learning to trust your judgment." With an effort she smiled up at him, albeit tremulously. How could she ever tell him how deeply grateful she was to have him living on her ranch? She said simply, "I'm glad you're here."

The shifting light suddenly revealed his expression, and Allie caught her breath.

His eyes were those of a hungry man.

"I don't want you," he said gruffly, "to be glad about anything I do. I don't want you to rely on me. I told you that before—you have to leave me alone." He jerked away, and Allie was amazed to sense a wildness in him.

"Leave you alone?" she cried, stung. "What have I done to crowd you? What have I done to make you run in the opposite direction?" All at once she was trembling. A charged silence vibrated between them. Allie was deeply aware of her smaller stature—of Dal's greater strength—his masculine scowl. He was silent, half-turned away. Aloof. "Damn you," she whispered. "I don't understand. *Answer* me."

"What have you done?" he repeated in a low, deep voice, facing her. She could see his expression again and something in his eyes was hot and dangerous. "You've just been you."

Reaching out with hard hands he yanked her flush against him. For a brief second he simply held her—one hand crushing the vulnerable area of her lower back—the other spearing into her hair. Then his lips crashed down upon hers in a kiss so fierce and uncontrollable Allie was thoroughly shocked.

Yet until that moment she hadn't admitted to herself how attracted she was to the taciturn cowboy. She hadn't admitted to stealing glances at the play of his hard, muscular back as he chopped firewood and dug post holes. At no time had she allowed herself to give in to the man's quietly simmering sensuality.

But she couldn't deny those things any longer.

Allie tasted mint and a trace of bourbon as Dal moved his mouth against hers. His lips were wet, demanding, scorching. Too intimate. She pushed against his chest, but with only a fraction of her normal resolve. The length of him pressed along her body was startling and exciting. His jeans scraped her legs, almost bare except for her pantyhose. Her breasts crushed against his chest in the open heavy coat. Through his thin shirt she could feel his heart surging and felt an answering thrill within.

Eroding faster than sand through an hourglass, her will to refuse him drained away. Dal was smart, he was capable. Those two qualities alone were enough to draw her. Add to that his manly strength, all six-foot-four of it, and Allie's customary reserve fragmented into the night air.

For a long stirring moment she merely accepted him. Then her fingers rose to touch his hair, skim over his nape. When he felt her hands on his face his mouth gentled, and she began, surprising herself, to kiss him back.

Kissing Dal, she discovered, was heaven. Running through a field of summer wheat. An exhilarating swim in the creek. Stormy winds. Wild thunder.

Never had she felt so consumed...so desperately wanted. The heady sensation of his desire for her spread liquid feminine languor through her limbs. She curled into him, trusting him to bear her weight, surrendering herself to his keeping for long delicious moments.

She hadn't realized his arms would feel so possessive and protective. She found the sensation addictive. For a long time she'd held on to the ranch essentially alone—but now she had a strong man to help her and guide her. And despite his denials he was helping and guiding. He wanted her.

The heat in her lower belly grew unbearable. She knew the first darts of fear at her own intensity. "Dal!" she gasped, wresting her lips free. His mouth took refuge along her brow, then pressed kisses on her cheeks, over her eyes, across her jaw.

"Dal!" she tried again, head spinning. "I can't do this. I can't—"

"Your hair smells so sweet," he muttered, burying his face in the long golden strands. "Like fresh-mown hay and bright flowers."

"I—I perfumed it," she said shakily, distracted.

"I know." He sought her neck with his lips. "God, I know. For Hunt. And you wore your hair down for him, too. Don't you think I noticed? Don't you know it drove me crazy, seeing you leave with him—knowing he was touching you?" He shuddered, crushing her against him so hard her feet came off the ground.

"Dal, he didn't!" she blurted. For some reason it was essential he know the truth. "He didn't touch me. Not—not that way."

Blazing into hers, his eyes studied her for an interminable moment. Then the air rushed out of him in a ragged sound. "Thank God." He set her down but didn't release her. In his fierce gaze she read deep hunger. Abiding loneliness. Torment.

Unable to resist, she ran gentle fingers over his hard mouth. "Dal, what's haunting you—no—don't deny it. I can sense some terrible pain eating at you. Talk to me . . . please."

Within seconds an unbreachable wall sprang between them. It happened so suddenly she was shocked. His face, taut with passion, transformed into forbidding lines of cold dismissal. His hold loosened, then fell away until his arms hung stiffly at his sides. Stepping back, he put a good two feet between them, and without his body warmth the chill night wind seemed to slice right through her. "This was a mistake," he said flatly.

Allie shivered. She wrapped her arms around herself and stared uncomprehendingly at the man who had just kissed her so thoroughly. "Yes," she agreed, her voice faint. Her lips were cold, her whole body was cold. "A mistake."

"I'll go into town tomorrow and check on prices for the posts and wire for the new section." He moved to the steps and struck out for the bunkhouse. "Let's forget about tonight," he said, face averted. "It never happened."

Chapter Five

Wanderlust. The urge to move on. The impulse to travel—
it was on him again. Dal felt the familiar longings and gritted his teeth. It was a two-year-old habit, this leaving whenever things got sticky. And for two years, each time it had
taken hold, he'd heeded the call.

But not this time.

The urge had come upon him once because the rancher
for whom he worked started relying too heavily on his skill
with animals; Dal hadn't liked that. At another spread, it
was because he was just one of many cowhands. It was a
smoothly run operation, they hadn't really needed him, and
he just moved on. There had been other places, other leave-
takings. But none had ever been prompted by a woman.

Allie was a woman who could drive a man away. She,
with her long, honey-colored hair, fierce blue eyes and sweet
body. There was danger in that kind of attraction.

She could also make a man want to stay on a long time.
Maybe too long.

Dal paced the length of the bunkhouse and back again, his boots making a steady ring on the bare floorboards. Would it be wise to stay on here? That he was needed, there was no doubt. Allie was going to fail without him. Maybe even *with* him. But at least if he did stay she'd have a fighting chance.

Rubbing a weary hand over his brow, Dal sighed. He wasn't sure what was right anymore. He'd lost the ability to judge—or to trust his instincts.

Sweet Lord, he was tired of making mistakes.

The words *a killing frost* could strike fear into the heart of any self-respecting rancher, and Allie Pearson was not immune. In a bad frost water tanks froze solid so the stock couldn't drink, and the covering of ice had to be chopped open each day. Animals weakened. Newborn calves froze to death.

Monday morning she listened with growing horror to the radio announcement, then watched morosely as her thermometer dropped degree by degree. She was glad Jessie had spent the night at the neighbor's house.

It was mid-morning and well below freezing. Dal let himself into the house without knocking. He shut the door against the high winds that invaded on his heels. "At least five or six heifers are ready to drop their calves," he told her in clipped tones. "I'll go out and bring 'em in close to the barn."

Allie nodded and wasted no time lamenting her bad fortune. "Pete and I'll come, too. I want to check on them myself. Besides, they might be hard to drive at this point."

Dal agreed and went out to the barn.

Because of the drought, Allie had been caught by surprise by the cold snap, although logically, she shouldn't have. She'd been so concerned by the lack of water that a frost hadn't occurred to her. Now that her cows were ready to deliver, it was a dangerous time on her ranch.

She drew on woolen long johns and several layers of clothing, topped by her father's sheepskin coat. Despite the layers, the cold wind screamed straight through her clothing to her skin.

"At least it's not snowing," Pete said jokingly, throwing a saddle on top of Sally, the mare Jed had foundered, but who'd recovered nicely under Dal's care.

Dal settled an Indian-print saddle blanket over his black gelding. "That's what I like about you, Pete," he remarked.

"What?" Pete pulled his baseball cap lower and blew on his hands.

"You're not too smart. The only thing you notice about a frost is that it's not snowing." Tightening his mount's cinch, Dal kept his expression bland, but Allie could see the glint of humor in his eyes. She knew he really liked Pete.

"Aw, Dal—"

"Come on, boy, you aren't wearing as much as Allie and I. Aren't you freezing your—" Dal glanced at Allie, then finished "—toes off?"

"Me?" Pete shrugged innocently and bared his teeth in a wide grin. "I don't know the meaning of the word *cold*. Why, this here little breeze ain't nothin'."

Allie glanced under the neck of Dal's horse at Pete and smiled at his affected drawl.

Pete went on, "Why, you don't suppose this is *cold*, do ya, Dal? You must be a real sissy. Now me, I've ridden out in weather so cold the cows gave icicles. Colder than a pawnbroker's smile. Colder 'n a mother-in-law's kiss."

Dal's laughter turned into a howl. "Why, you're never gonna know what a mother-in-law's kiss feels like, boy! You're too ugly and stupid to catch a wife. Besides, you aren't half-grown."

Pete was unperturbed by Dal's ribbing. He stuck out his developing chest and slanted a glance full of male bravado at his tormentor. "Don't you worry about me. When I get me a wife, I'll be able to do my, uh, duty by her."

Dal chuckled and Allie pursed her lips at the innuendo. She slipped the headstall over her mare and said, "You're far too young to be thinking about wives and such. You don't even graduate from high school for two more months."

"Yeah, and after that I'll be free! No more school."

Allie smiled, but was surprised when Dal said, "What about college? A man needs a degree these days to make anything out of himself."

"Aw, I don't need college. I'll just work on this ranch or another. I like cowboyin'."

Dal shook his head stubbornly. He wasn't smiling any longer. "Not good enough. I'll never let any son of mine go on without . . . what is it?"

Allie gasped and stood stock-still. She stared at him and asked tentatively, "You—you've got a son?"

"Hell, no, I don't have a son! I've never even been married. I just mean *if* I did, he'd go to college."

Patting her horse's neck, Allie allowed herself a small smile of satisfaction. "My, my," she said. "What do you know? However did that little bit of information escape those tight lips?"

Dal looked slightly abashed and stern at the same time. "It's no secret."

"No? Any other *un*secrets you want to confide today?"

Deigning not to answer, he mounted with the others. But Allie saw no evidence of anger on his features as she had last night after he kissed her.

He'd told her to forget it, and indeed, he acted as if he had. But she hadn't. Even now she could still feel the wild flare of arousal that shot through her when he'd held her for those few brief moments. She could hear his ragged breathing in her ear.

His kiss had moved their relationship into a realm she didn't need or want. He'd made her consciously aware of him as a living, breathing person—and not just an employee. He'd made her aware of him as a man.

Of course her unexpected response to him had been the chance product of several merging events. Already at maximum stress with worry about the ranch and taking proper care of Jessie, Allie had to deal with the new shock of a possibly serious cattle disease.

Exhausted and frightened when Dal had reached for her, it was mere coincidence that she'd needed affection right then. Everyone wanted to be held now and again, Allie reasoned, everyone needed comfort. She'd simply taken a moment of her life to turn toward his warmth.

Allie set her jaw and kicked her mare into a hard gallop. As she passed Dal, she felt his surprised glance, but she didn't care.

Dal caught up with her as she finally slowed. "What's your hurry?"

She shrugged her shoulders, stiff in the cold. Despite her rationalizations about their embrace, she still couldn't quite forget his touch, his words of praise. She couldn't forget his scent; he smelled of home and horse and winter sun. *Damn him.* "I felt like a run," she told him. "I guess I can run a horse over my own land if I feel like it."

"Yes, ma'am." His eyes narrowed. "Anything you say, boss."

"Good," she answered, unable to help needling him. "I like a respectful attitude in my employees. See that you keep it." *And don't kiss me anymore!*

Nose in the air, Allie forced her horse to wheel on its hind legs and head off at an angle toward the east pasture.

They brought in six heifers heavy with calves and began a round-the-clock patrol of the pastures.

The following day a pickup she recognized as belonging to Lubbock Feed Barn eased past the mailbox and came to a stop before her.

Tricia, the owner's daughter, climbed out of the cab and set her high-heeled pumps gingerly on the gravel drive. Allie shook her head at the unlikely shoes and went forward. Tricia always wore the tightest jeans, the silliest footwear and the most makeup of any teenager around, although Allie knew her to be a good-hearted girl.

"I brought out the hay you ordered," she informed Allie, turning up her coat collar against the cold and staring off in the direction of Slade's land.

"Thanks, Tricia," Allie said. "I'll have the men unload it."

"Men?" Tricia said with half her attention. "You have more than the one hand you brought to town last week?"

"That was Dal," she said. "But I have Pete, too."

"Oh, Pete." Tricia resumed scanning Slade's property.

Riding up at that moment, Dal and Pete pushed two more cows into the holding pen and dismounted. Allie told Dal what the vet had said and then asked him and Pete to unload the hay.

"Hi, Tricia," Pete said to the girl. She'd pulled a nail file from her back pocket and had begun working on her long nails.

"Hi." She barely glanced up. "Can you hurry? I've got to get back."

"Sure. Why don't you have a seat in the barn where it's warmer? Dal and I'll get that hay down quick for you." As he spoke he whipped off his baseball cap and turned the brim around and around in his hands.

Tricia stuffed her file back into her pocket and resumed her study of the neighboring lands. "Naw, I'll wait out here."

At Pete's eager solicitousness, Allie lifted a brow. "Pete," she said, "back up the truck as close as you can to the hay loft. But watch out for that old hitching post." She indicated a cast-iron post decorated with a figure of a horse head.

"Okay, Allie." He ran to perform the chore, but in his haste somehow managed to back the truck squarely into the iron horse head. The tailgate clanked as it collided, and the post tilted crazily to the side. Allie groaned.

Tricia laughed.

Blushing furiously, Pete stammered apologies, pulled the truck forward and surveyed the damage. All the while peals of Tricia's laughter rang out and Pete's face got redder. "I don't know what's so funny," he got out finally.

"You!" She pointed at him with one hand, her other covered her mouth. "That was so...so *stupid!*"

Pete ground his teeth. "Stupid, huh? I guess you think you're so smart—you never make mistakes?"

"Not *that* dumb. Boy, you get the award. I can't wait to tell everybody at the store. They'll laugh their heads off!"

Allie was about to intervene when she thought better of it. The two teenagers should work out their own problems. There was plenty to do without standing around playing referee, so she lifted one of the sacks of grain Tricia had also brought and lugged it into the barn. Their voices carried to her inside.

Pete sounded good and mad now. "Why do you have to tell everybody? When you act dumb, I don't go spilling it to the world."

"That's because I never do anything ridiculous." Tricia sniffed with great superiority.

"No? What about the way you moon around after Slade Hunt? That's pretty ridiculous. Why, he's got to be ten or eleven years older than you, girl. What makes you think he'd ever be interested in you anyway?"

Tricia gasped. "I'm not a—a *girl* any more, Pete. I'm a woman—eighteen years old—and don't you forget it. A whole year older than you."

Pete spat onto the frozen ground. "Your birthday was last month, wasn't it? I saw those balloons at the feed barn. Well, mine's in March. You're only two months older."

"Well, Slade *is* interested in me. A *lot*."

"I'm not so sure. Besides, what do you see in him?"

"A boy like you could hardly understand. Slade is a grown-up, a successful businessman. What are you—just a stable boy!"

"I'm not! I do a man's work here. Why, I work right alongside of Dal—gathering cattle, stringing fence—"

"You *do* muck out stables, don't you, though? I don't suppose a successful man like Slade stomps around in the manure at his own ranch. He pays some nobody like you to do it."

Allie had heard enough. She came out of the barn, intent on yelling at them both when she realized Pete had already stalked off. Tricia was merely digging through her purse for gum.

"Tricia," Allie said. "That was cruel."

The girl had the grace to look mildly abashed—yet her mouth still turned down mutinously. She lowered her eyes. "Maybe it was, but he asked for it."

"Well, I wasn't going to interfere between you two, but I think now maybe I'd best." Allie leaned a hip against the truck fender. "Pete's right about something—Slade is considerably older—and more experienced."

"I don't care." She slid a stick of gum into her mouth.

"You should. Don't you know a man like him can read a young girl like a book? He knows you've got a crush on him, Trish." She straightened and put a hand on the girl's arm. Softly she said, "He's just not a forever kind of guy. He's shallow. A ladies' man."

When Tricia didn't reply, Allie let her hand fall away and her bitter smile turned inward. "He's an attractive man, I know. But we women have to watch out for ourselves. It's those kind that break our hearts when they eventually leave us for something or someone better."

With her head still bent, Tricia peeked up, and Allie knew the teenager was wondering about her past. To forestall questions she suggested, "Pete's growing into a fine man. He'll be the sort that will stand by a woman."

"Pete's just a kid."

Shaking her head, Allie pulled on her heavy gloves and slashed a hay hook into the first bale. Dal came out of the barn, pulling on his own gloves. "I'll unload the hay, Allie."

She frowned at him. "I can do it. Don't you think I'm strong enough?"

"I *know* you're strong enough. But I'm stronger. I can do it faster and more efficiently. There's plenty other work for you around here." He waited for her to move away, gloved hands on lean hips.

She gave in ungraciously. "All right. Just so long as you understand that I *can* do it."

He said nothing, merely waited.

Allie stood back and watched for a moment while Dal came forward and began hefting the heavy bales. She noted the play of his muscles beneath his yoked shirt and admitted he was far more capable.

It wasn't the first time he'd come upon her performing a difficult chore and taken over. She always reacted huffily, but he never relented, calmly pointing out his own superior technique or strength, and then suggesting another, lighter task for her. Before Dal, no one had ever noticed the strain the heavy work put on her. No one had made her load easier. Though she would protest, in her most secret heart she admitted she liked it.

And Dal was proving an adept midwife. He'd assisted several of her cows with difficult deliveries—she'd witnessed other births enough times to recognize his skill.

One evening at dusk, a weary-eyed Dal drove a laboring cow into the corral close to the house. Dal had been on horseback since well before dawn, checking out new calves, then winter feeding and stringing new fence along the front side of her property. Allie knew he must be exhausted, but he never complained.

When the cow trotted into the corral and through the connecting door into a warm indoor stall, she immediately lay down and groaned.

"Is she all right?" Allie asked, following inside and closing the door against the cold wind. Jessie peered from behind the slats of the stall.

"She'll be all right," he said curtly. "But whatever made you buy Charolais bulls? These calves are so big, some of the Hereford cows can hardly deliver them!"

"Charolais beef is lower in fat," she defended. "With the new nutrition-conscious market, I thought the Charolais-Hereford cross was a good idea. I...uh, didn't think too much about calving problems."

Dal dismounted and proceeded to disinfect his hands and arms, then apply the obstetrical lubricant Allie kept in stock at this time of year. He examined the cow closely. "The calf is in a good position, belly-down and coming frontwards, but one leg is wedged behind the head."

Jessie's round eyes grew even rounder. "Is the cow gonna have a baby, Mom?"

"Yes, honey."

"What's Dal doing to her?" She pointed at the man and beast both kneeling in the straw.

"He's helping her have the baby. Now hush and you can watch if you stay quiet."

Jessie nodded solemnly.

Loath to distract Dal as he worked between the cow's contractions, Allie was gratified when he kept up a low running commentary. "I'm shifting the calf's shoulder and upper arm so I can straighten it." He grunted with effort, then said, "I've got the hoof now. It's coming forward."

Moments later the leg was freed and the tan-yellow colored calf delivered soon after. "Oh, look, Jess," Allie breathed, awed as always by the miracle of birth. "Isn't she something?"

Jessie stuck her head between the stall slats. "Can I touch her?"

"Not yet, honey." Dal stood back and made sure the cow accepted the calf.

Allie studied him. "Pete's been telling me about your knowledge of animals—he's just about got you pegged for a hero."

Dal smiled. "Pete's a good kid."

"You sure are good with the cattle, though." She looked at him narrowly.

"A cowboy's got to be a jack-of-all-trades, that's for sure," he said, disappointing her. He stepped out of the stall and stripped off his shirt. At the sink he washed himself. Lathering his arms and chest, Dal worked at cleaning off the lubricant while Allie gave him a sidelong inspection.

The barn's low lighting slid warmly over the hard swells of his biceps and thick raised veins that started at his wrists and snaked up his forearms. She noticed the pelt of dark hair that covered his developed pectorals and arrowed down to disappear into his jeans. A quick, heated flash spurted through her as she remembered what it felt like to be held against his solid frame. He was truly a big man. He'd probably be big all over.

Blushing furiously, she turned her back and crouched beside Jessie, waiting for him to towel off. After watching Dal's gentle skill and patience, Allie was struck anew by the fact that Dal had killed someone. He even admitted it, although he refused to share details.

Somehow the notion of anything other than self-defense or an accident was not believable. The Dal she knew would never intentionally harm someone. She kept her back turned and longed to know the truth. Would he ever trust her enough to tell her? By this time, she knew she would never call the sheriff. It had become more important to keep Dal— just for the ranch, she told herself.

"I'm glad we were able to get a healthy calf out of this one, Allie," he said.

"Yes." She didn't turn around.

"Because I've got bad news."

Allie was alarmed by the reluctance in his voice. She heard the sounds of fabric rustling and guessed he was pulling on his shirt. "Well?"

Slowly he told her, "Pete and I found one of your new bulls caught in a tangle of barbed wire."

On her knees she whirled. "Is he hurt? Did you get him out?"

By the look on his face she already knew the answer. "I'm sorry, Allie. But we hadn't seen him for two days because he'd wandered down a wash at the far end of your property. He's dead."

Allie felt her face crumpling and bowed her head so he wouldn't see. All that she'd fought for, all her work and worry—would it be for nothing? One of her blooded bulls was gone. Her fingers on Jessie's shoulders tightened, and the girl turned instinctively to hug her mother. Sitting on her heels, Allie hugged her back and fought tears.

The scuffle of booted feet in the barn doorway brought her head up. Slade appeared. "You lost a bull, Allie?"

She nodded, not trusting her voice yet.

For once the arrogant rancher seemed subdued. "That's rough."

Dal barely acknowledged his presence.

"If there's anything I can do to help . . . ?" Slade walked toward Allie and when she stood, put a hand on her shoulder.

She sighed. "I don't think so."

"Maybe you'd like to try artificial insemination—have your vet over to take some samples from my bulls come summer?"

Allie's eyes shot to his face. "You—you mean it?"

"Sure. I've got Charolais, just like yours."

With a darting glance at Dal, Allie asked tentatively, "Maybe we could use the Hereford bulls?"

"No problem." He squeezed her shoulder and Allie didn't shrug off the reassuring gesture. In her relief she barely noticed Dal's frowning glance on Slade's caressing hand. "You've had a hard year, that's for sure. How about coming out with me tonight—take your mind off your worries?"

"What?" she said absently, thinking of the wonderful opportunity he'd offered her. "Oh, no thank you. I've got a pot of beef stew simmering."

"I like stew." Slade stroked her shoulder and smiled, his brown eyes gleaming in the dim light.

"I don't like stew." Jessie looked straight up at the rancher, for once her face devoid of its customary smile.

Slade was not put off by her attitude. He leaned down and placed his face close to hers. "Then I'll eat your share."

Shaking herself, Allie said, "Um, Slade, are you asking to stay for dinner?"

His wide grin was in direct contrast to Dal's darkening scowl. "Stay for dinner? I surely will, thank you. Such an unexpected invitation."

Jessie clung tight to her mother's hand. "You can't sit in my place," she told him.

"Jessie!" Allie said, surprised by her daughter's rudeness. "We show good manners to our neighbors."

Slade laughed heartily. "Don't scold her, Mama. There's nothing wrong with a spirited female. That's how I like 'em."

From across the room where Dal was putting away tools, there came a noise that sounded like a snort. Allie looked at Dal sharply, but his expression was bland.

"Well, let's go in to eat, then. You can wash up while I heat a loaf of sourdough." She tugged on Jessie's hand and led her into the house.

Jessie continued to be uncharacteristically contrary to Slade—right up until the time he said, "You really don't like stew, do you, little one? You haven't eaten any. But I'll bet I know what you'd like."

"What?"

"A pony of your own?"

Allie looked at Slade in surprise and wondered how he'd chanced upon the one thing dear to her daughter's heart.

"A spotted one," Jessie told him matter-of-factly, as if everyone must know her fondest wish.

Dal had spent most of the meal glaring at Slade, to which Slade appeared blissfully oblivious. Yet now he spoke up. "Jess is working hard to earn money so she can buy a little Shetland."

Allie felt Slade's eyes on her face as he said, "Well, now, we'll have to see about getting her one."

"Really?" Jessie squealed and bounced in her chair. "I can buy the pony. I've got lots of money saved."

"Is that right?" Slade's dark brows rose in surprise.

"I'll show you!" Jessie slid off her stool and raced to her room. Allie smiled indulgently as the little girl came speeding back, her pink ceramic piggy bank held in both hands. "See all my pennies! I had sixteen but Dal gave me a lot more—like about twenty. Right, Dal?"

Dal put both elbows on the table. As he looked at Slade, there was challenge in his eyes. "Right."

Allie didn't understand Dal's animosity, and the truth was she avoided analyzing it. She had enough problems.

Slade burst into laughter. He shook his head at the child. "You've got to be kidding. At this rate you'll be an old, gray woman by the time you've got enough."

The sinking expression on Jessie's face tore at Allie's heart. The little girl walked slowly back to her room and Allie rounded on Slade. "How could you?" she demanded.

Dal stood, rising to his full height. His frown was threatening but his voice was soft. "Jessie's only four years old— she doesn't understand about money yet."

"Don't worry about it." Slade said, getting up to clear his empty stew bowl. "I'm plannin' on buyin' her one, anyway."

Allie's first reaction was surprised pleasure. Her daughter would get the wish she most wanted, something Allie couldn't give her. Jessie could learn to ride on a small, calm pony. She'd experience the joy and responsibility of caring for her own animal.

But in seconds Allie's pleasure faded. Slade had offered so much, she already felt beholden to him. What would he expect in return? What could she actually give?

"No," she heard herself saying, "Jessie's going to save her money until she *can* buy herself that pony. It may be a few more years and it won't be blooded stock, but she'll do it. When I can, I'll slip a couple of dollars into her piggy to speed it along. Dal's already given her several handfuls of change." She nodded at her silent employee.

Twisting to face Dal, Slade let his dark-eyed gaze assess the man. "He has, has he? Well, I can do better." Setting down his plate, he dug into his rear pocket, fished out a new leather wallet and proceeded to pile twenty-dollar bills on the table.

Allie put her hand over the steadily mounting pile and pushed it back toward Slade. "If you want to help, then put your money away and just encourage her. We all need something to work for—look forward to."

A fleeting grimace crossed Slade's face, then he stuffed the money back. He said, "I'll help with the dishes, Allie. I'm a good washer."

"Really?" Allie smiled at him in delight. She hated washing dishes. Even Dal had never offered to help in the kitchen. "You're on. I'll dry."

"I'll help, Allie," Dal said suddenly, getting to his feet. After his long silence, he sounded unusually aggressive.

"Naw," Slade returned, gathering plates. "You go sit with the kid." He indicated Jessie with a careless motion.

Silently Allie beseeched Dal. For a long moment she thought he'd argue. During dinner the undercurrents between the two men made her nervous. Finally he gave her a short nod. "But I forgot to do something in the bunkhouse. I'll be back in a few minutes."

There was nothing in the bunkhouse but solitude—something Dal desperately needed right then. Tonight he felt as tightly strung as a steer on the end of a rope. Inside the cold, dusty room Dal closed the door and leaned against an exposed wood stud. From there he had a clear view out the window to the open pasture. Cold moonlight glinted on the rail posts and glowed silvery on the backs of the cattle. At his side, his hands clenched.

He was starting to feel proprietary about Allie. Jealous of Slade Hunt. And he had no right. Fortunately, no one knew him in these parts; he was only the anonymous "Dal," so there would be no censure for her in employing him. The censure came from inside him.

Hating to do it, he deliberately allowed the memories to wash over him. For Allie's sake, he had to remember who and what he was.

Pouring into his mind came memories of red-hot rage for the man he'd killed. Images of a strength that matched his own accompanied by a cruel smile and mocking laugh. Dal had never felt such intense anger toward another human being.

He remembered being surprised to see the gray-blue metal of a gun barrel in the man's fist. For the first time he'd experienced fear—not for himself—for others. The madman waved the weapon overhead, shouting obscenities and threats. Dal made a lunge for the gun, struggled for it. Then his sister's screams...gunshots...the man's expression of surprise as he realized he'd been shot...the slumping of his weight into Dal's arms.

On and on his sister had screamed, the shrill cries continuing until Dal slammed his fists over his ears and squeezed his eyes shut.

Still leaning against the wooden stud, Dal straightened and shuddered. Clammy sweat beaded on his forehead. He opened his eyes and faced himself and what he'd become. Or tried to.

It took a solid fifteen minutes to bring himself under enough control to return to the house.

Just inside the doorway, he glanced into the kitchen and saw a homey scene. Jessie was playing contentedly on the floor with her pots and pans, and Hunt had his hands on Allie's back and nape, massaging her, while *she* washed dishes.

The breath whistled through Dal's teeth in an angry hiss. Neither Allie nor Slade had seen him—they were too engrossed in each other. They certainly didn't need a third wheel around, so he backed outside, closing the door quietly behind him.

The decision was made.

In the bunkhouse he worked quickly. There wasn't much to do, he had so few belongings. After gathering his bedroll and stuffing his clothes into saddlebags, he went into the barn and saddled Black Jack.

"It's time to head out, boy," he told the gelding, leading the ebony-dark horse into the equally dark evening. Man and horse and night blended together. By morning he'd be far way. Far enough to forget about Allie Pearson and her problems. Far enough to lose the memory of her golden hair and blue eyes and bright smile.

Dal swung up, saddle leather creaking as he did so. He didn't know how far he'd have to go to forget everything about Allie. But he knew one thing: he was going to keep moving until he got there.

Chapter Six

"He's gone," Allie breathed to herself as she stood shivering in the bunkhouse doorway. When Dal didn't come up for breakfast, she wondered if he'd lost track of time or perhaps was still out feeding the cattle. Finally she'd come looking.

At a glance it was obvious he'd abandoned her. His bedroll was gone, the small chest of drawers where he'd kept his meager belongings gaped open . . . empty.

On a sudden thought, she wheeled and raced to the barn. At the first stall she skidded to a halt in the loose straw and peered over the door. Black Jack was gone, too.

The drifter had moved on.

Thrusting her hands into the front pockets of her blue jeans, Allie glared down at her scuffed boots. Well, she'd deserved this! He'd warned her—several times—not to count on him. He'd told her he would leave at some point. So why was she so bitterly disappointed? Why did she feel like lying down in a pile of straw and sobbing?

All the bitter emotions of Paxton's abandonment came rushing back, swamping Allie. She'd been so young, so trusting. Nothing in her sheltered upbringing had prepared her for the wiles of a silver-tongued man intent on using her for easy sex.

Because that's all it had been.

For him anyway. So blinded by his incredibly handsome face and seductive ways, Allie had had little chance against him. She'd loved him—or thought so. Having sex was something two people did who loved each other. Surrendering to Paxton, sliding onto the back of his motorcycle when he'd wanted to move on had been a natural consequence of her love.

To her everlasting shame, she'd discovered the hard way that having sex and making love were two entirely different things. She would never forget the expression on her father's face as she'd made the decision to take off with Paxton. Her mother had been disbelieving, horrified, panic-stricken that their sweet, biddable, nineteen-year-old daughter could even consider roaring off on a wickedly black Harley with a shiftless rebel like Dwight Paxton.

But she had. And she'd gotten what she deserved. Now she was older, wiser.

Suddenly Allie started laughing. Wiser? Hadn't she almost made a similar mistake with Dal?

Squatting in the straw, Allie laughed, dry-eyed, then dropped her face into her hands. Would she never learn? Obviously her instincts were flawed. She had better learn, at least, not to trust them. When it came to men, her decision-making processes were skewed.

With great effort she forced herself to stand and look around the barn, remind herself miserably of the work still waiting, Dal or no Dal.

Outside she heard the engine of Pete's sedan. She remained rooted, unable to summon the energy to greet him.

He came in and noticed immediately that Dal's black gelding was not in his stall.

"Where's Dal?"

"Gone."

"Oh. He took a day off?"

"Yeah." She let out a bitter laugh that held no humor.
"He took a day off, all right."

For some reason Pete missed the sarcasm in her voice and
cheerfully collected up a hay hook. "Well, he knows I'll take
care of the feeding. He's been working hard. A man's got to
take time off now and again," he informed her.

But he won't be coming back, she wanted to scream.

Pete started to whistle as he worked, grating on Allie's
nerves. To keep her hands busy, she grabbed the handles of
a wheelbarrow and pushed it to the haystack.

"I'll do this job, Allie," Pete told her with a wide grin.
"Since I've been working with Dal, I'm a little stronger
now." Playfully he flexed the muscle of one biceps, and Allie attempted to smile. Normally she'd have teased him, but
at the moment teasing was beyond her.

"Okay, Pete. If you're hungry, you can come up to the
house for breakfast."

He halted mid-stride, the hay hook dangling from his
hand. Hopefully he asked, "Flapjacks?"

"Sure." She shrugged and turned away. Dal had always
asked for her fluffy flapjacks.

At the house she mixed batter and poured it onto the
griddle. Jessie wandered in, dragging her teddy bear and
rubbing her eyes. When Pete came up to the house, Allie
gave each a plate.

Gulping coffee, Pete took a second to glance at her. "You
aren't eating?"

Arms crossed beneath her breasts, Allie let her gaze wander over to the window. "Nah. I'm not hungry."

"They're yummy," Jessie pronounced, pouring too much syrup over her small stack and getting some on her pajamas.

"That's good, honey." Allie wiped up a few spilled droplets of syrup and watched the two eat.

By lunchtime she still wasn't hungry, but her gaze kept going to the window. When she caught herself actually going out onto the porch for the fourth time to peer down the road—for God knew who—she got mad.

"He's not coming back, Allison Pearson," she muttered darkly. "So just forget about him." At dinner she recognized the dull ache of hunger in her stomach and forced down some fried chicken and mashed potatoes. She washed dishes and read Jessie a story and straightened the house, all the while wishing she'd never set eyes on the maverick cowboy named only "Dal." She wished she'd never let him make a place for himself on her ranch.

At bedtime of the interminable day, she turned off her bedside lamp and pulled her patchwork quilt over her to shut out the chill. The long sleepless night was even more interminable, but she managed a light doze toward dawn.

Within the hour she dragged herself out of bed, realizing that Pete would need her help with the morning chores. She could at least feed the horses in the barn, clean stalls and spread mash for the laying hens.

As she pulled on dusty jeans and twisted her hair into a haphazard braid, she wondered at her lack of enthusiasm. Before Dal's arrival and during his stay, she'd begun each day in a flurry of activity. Now all she felt was lethargic and hopeless.

It angered her that she had begun to rely so much on one man. And not just on his work. She'd enjoyed his company, admired his skill, liked talking with him. Many times she'd sought him out on the merest excuse, just to be with him. He'd always been welcoming—pleased to see her.

Allie's anger at Dal's defection deepened. Not into the
white-hot furnace of rage—but into a slow-burning coal of
regret and helpless loss. As she quietly let herself outside and
walked to the barn, Allie forced herself to recognize the
emotion for what it truly was. She was sick at heart.

The problem with women was they were too damn fickle.
And he was too stupid to learn. Back in Allie's bunkhouse
at 4:30 a.m., Dal jerked on his boots and cursed the world
in general.

Buttoning a flannel shirt, he pulled on his jacket. He set
his dark Stetson low over his eyes and hoped the wind
wouldn't blow the darn thing off today; it was a damned
nuisance getting off his horse to retrieve it. Closing the door,
he accidentally shut it on his thumb.

Dal cursed again. Everything seemed to be bothering him.
After the long grueling evening two nights ago spent listen-
ing to Slade Hunt make boastful promises to Allie, and then
watching her eyes widen, impressed, he longed to slam his
fist into a wall, sore thumb and all. Or maybe kick something so hard it broke.

Even little Jessie had disappointed him. He could tell she
hadn't liked or trusted Hunt at first, and he'd inwardly ap-
plauded the girl's perception. But when Hunt had offered
to buy her that pony, she'd gone all hopeful-eyed and eager
toward him.

Women! They were all fickle.

Dal swore again and stomped toward Allie's barn. The
long night spent outdoors with only his horse for company
and a stick of beef jerky for dinner, instead of one of Allie's fine home-cooked meals, hadn't improved his mood
any. But in a matter of hours after riding out he'd realized
running away, at least this time, was wrong.

A blast of morning air hit him full in the face and he
paused, taking a minute to adjust to the cold. Gray clouds

hung heavily overhead, and the chill wind swept past him to the open pasture. He shivered, grimly recalling that he had to take an ax out to the water tanks and break ice.

He shrugged almost philosophically, beginning the hated process of loading hay bales onto the truck. This was his job now. He couldn't go back—back to the home and work he'd known since birth. With a man's death on his conscience, deliberate or not, he'd earned the lifelong animosity of his sister, the devastating disappointment of his father and the alienation of his two brothers.

Dal grunted and heaved bale after eighty-pound bale into the truck, welcoming the aching muscles that came with the exhausting work. It was the only thing he'd found to keep his agonizing past at bay. That, and a pair of wide eyes, as clear and blue as a Texas sky.

He didn't hear her footsteps until she was almost upon him. She hadn't seen him yet, either, he could tell by the way her head was tucked into her chest and her arms were wrapped tightly about her middle, as if she were hugging herself.

Coming to an abrupt halt at the truck, she spotted him, shock written clearly across her face. He paused in stacking hay, saying nothing. Her gaze went past him to where Black Jack was visible in the stall, slowly chewing hay. After looking briefly at him again, she swung her head around and narrowed her eyes at the bunkhouse.

For once he knew exactly what she was thinking. She was wondering if his clothing had been put back inside the drawers he'd left open. She was wondering if he was back to stay. Still, he said nothing.

Their eyes met, and Allie's surprised expression faded into acceptance. A small smile appeared at the corners of her mouth; he couldn't help returning it. Silently she went about feeding the hens. But her smile remained.

* * *

"It's anaplasmosis, all right," Paul Radovitch, the gray-ing veterinarian, announced to Allie. He put his thermo-meter and stethoscope into a large bag and faced her, the fatigue of his long hours etching lines into his aging face. He'd examined the four cows Dal had brought into the holding pen and shook his head. "Lab results confirm it. The good news is, I don't think many of your cows are in-fected. We could keep this a small problem."

Allie felt fresh hope. "How do you suppose they got it? Dal said there are lots of ways."

"Have you brought in any new stock lately?" When she shook her head, he asked, "Done any branding or inocu-lating yet?" Again she shook her head. "Well," he went on, "it's early yet for tick season. Still, we've had a warm win-ter up until this week. I think we'd best concentrate imme-diately on treatment."

"Okay." She drew in a breath, relieved this wouldn't be another setback.

"It's lucky that I've got a new supply of tetracycline right here so we can start treatment," the doctor said. "If you'll send your man to me I'll instruct him about separating the sick stock from the healthy."

"Right." Allie waved to Dal where he was just riding in and decided to check on Jessie in the house while the vet spoke with Dal. Ten minutes later when she returned, the vet was pulling out of the driveway and Dal was inspecting the bottles of medicine. "Dal!" she cried. "Why is Doc Ra-dovitch leaving?"

He glanced at her sideways. "He left the medications with me. I'll handle the treatment."

"He's explained how to do everything already?" she ex-claimed in disbelief. She'd figured the doctor would be here at least an hour or so treating the cattle.

"Yeah."

NO RISK, NO OBLIGATION TO BUY ... NOW OR EVER!

CASINO JUBILEE

"Scratch'n Match" Game

Here's how to play:

1. Peel off label from front cover. Place it in space provided at right. With a coin, carefully scratch off the silver box. This makes you eligible to receive two or more free books, and possibly other gifts, depending upon what is revealed beneath the scratch-off area.

2. You'll receive brand-new Silhouette Romance™ novels. When you return this card, we'll rush you the books and gifts you qualify for ABSOLUTELY FREE!

3. If we don't hear from you, every month we'll send you 6 additional novels to read and enjoy months before they are available in bookstores. You can return them and owe nothing but if you decide to keep them, you'll pay only $2.25* per book, a saving of 44¢ each off the cover price. There is **no** extra charge for postage and handling. There are **no** hidden extras.

4. When you join the Silhouette Reader Service™, you'll get our subscribers-only newsletter, as well as additional free gifts from time to time just for being a subscriber!

5. You must be completely satisfied. You may cancel at any time simply by sending us a note or a shipping statement marked "cancel" or by returning any shipment to us at our cost.

YOURS FREE!

This lovely heart-shaped box is richly detailed with cut-glass decorations, perfect for holding a precious memento or keepsake—and it's yours absolutely free when you accept our no-risk offer.

CASINO JUBILEE
"Scratch'n Match" Game

SCRATCH HERE

PLACE LABEL HERE

?

CHECK CLAIM CHART BELOW FOR YOUR FREE GIFTS!

YES! I have placed my label from the front cover in the space provided above and scratched off the silver box. Please send me all the gifts for which I qualify. I understand I am under no obligation to purchase any books, as explained on the opposite page.

(U-SIL-R-11/92) 215 CIS AGND

Name _____

Address _____ Apt. _____

City _____ State _____ Zip _____

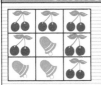

CASINO JUBILEE CLAIM CHART	
🍒🍒🍒 🍒🍒🍒	WORTH 4 FREE BOOKS, FREE HEART-SHAPED CURIO BOX PLUS MYSTERY BONUS GIFT
🍒🔔🍒	WORTH 3 FREE BOOKS PLUS MYSTERY GIFT
🔔🔔🍒	WORTH 2 FREE BOOKS CLAIM N° 1528

▼ DETACH AND MAIL CARD TODAY! ▼

SILHOUETTE "NO RISK" GUARANTEE

▼ DETACH AND MAIL CARD TODAY! ▼

For the first time she faced him with open suspicion. "You sure are a quick study."

He shrugged.

Hands on hips, she felt an almost overpowering urge to bombard him with questions. It was becoming all too obvious that he must have once owned property—been a working rancher himself. But why all the secrecy? Why had he placed her under the unnecessary edict to withhold any questions? The mystery was beginning to get to her.

Even so, she was loath to offend him by crossing the boundary he'd set. Especially when she recalled his violent reaction each time she'd questioned him. She could see by the way he handled the hypodermic needle and bottles of medications that he was no stranger to them—but she supposed it wasn't really so important she know of his past. What should matter to her was his present, and his present was serving to maintain her ranch.

Just then Dal leaned over the table, and the silver medallion that hung around his neck fell free from his shirt. "Where'd you get that?" she blurted before she could stop the words.

He glanced up warily and noted the direction of her gaze. His hand closed around the jewelry. "My father," he replied. "He gave one to me and to each of my brothers when we turned eighteen. Sort of a coming-of-age gift, I guess."

"Who are your brothers?" She waited, hardly daring to breathe and hoping he wouldn't blow up.

He smiled crookedly. "Let's just say they're cowboys, too."

"You don't see them much, do you?"

At that he bowed his head over the medallion. "No. It's been two years."

Eyes widening, Allie was about to remark that if she had been lucky enough to have siblings, two years would never pass before they would visit. But she caught the subtle closing of Dal's expression and knew better than to say it. Instead her own hand dropped to her belt buckle.

"I see you've got a trophy buckle," Dal said. "Mind if I take a look?"

She answered by letting her hand fall away. While he bent to examine the silver etching of a bucking horse and the words National Finals Rodeo and the year, she forced herself to remain still.

With his head breast-high, Allie could see the fine weathered lines at the corners of his eyes, testimony to years of outdoor work. His thick, black hair beneath his dark Stetson hat was wind-tossed and glossy. She wondered what it would be like to run her fingers through the dark waves. At that moment he looked up.

"It's a handsome buckle." He waited, his gaze on her face, and she knew he was asking where she'd gotten it.

"My father," she supplied. "He won it the year before I was born. Bareback bronc riding. I wear it to remind me of him, his strength and his courage."

Dal's heavy brows rose and he whistled low. "Well, I'll be damned. Your father must have been quite a man." Still bent over, with a long index finger he traced the outline of the horse. "I'll let you in on something. I've never won a rodeo trophy."

"I don't care," she replied without thinking. She only cared about *him*.

Their gazes met in a long, timeless exchange. She liked the way his sooty lashes framed his green eyes. She liked the way he looked at her—treated her with respect—took over the harder tasks. There wasn't any way he could possibly work harder than he did, and intuitively she knew he was doing it for her.

Slowly Dal straightened, his hand still at her waist on the buckle. His fingers brushed her stomach and she felt her muscles contract. The moment couldn't have been more intimate if he'd stroked her breast.

A curious, sudden blush flooded her cheeks. Filled with a strange agitation she refused to identify, she stepped aside and his hand fell away. "I guess you'd better get started on those cows."

His hand had fallen away, but his gaze had not. "I'll take care of your cattle for you, Allie," he told her softly. And she stared back despite her blush, for somehow it sounded as if he was promising to take care of *her*.

Allie's hands began to tremble.

It was a good thing he strode away then, because she never knew what she might have done, had he stayed a moment longer. With some shock she realized that she was vulnerable to this man in a way she hadn't been since Paxton had abandoned her—pregnant and penniless—in a backwater honky-tonk somewhere south of San Antonio.

The fact that Dal behaved in a manner totally at odds with what he said mattered little to Allie. Paxton had heaped pretty words of love on her on a regular basis, but when their romantic flight had palled and she'd turned up with child, he'd wished her luck, blew her a kiss and climbed onto the back of his motorcycle.

Actions speak louder than words. It was an axiom she'd learned the hard way, and well. Despite Dal's insistence to the contrary, he did care for her. He had returned, hadn't he, after his disappearance? He'd come back. Allie had seen genuine caring in each chore he undertook—from shouldering her share of work to the unhurried attention he paid to Jessie.

Nor for a single second could she forget the shattering passion of his kiss.

Dal cared for her all right, and he wanted her. At the same time, she realized, he didn't *want* to want her. In his past and in his head echoed some agonizing memory, some wrong never righted. She was beginning to understand that the aching wound was a cycle that might go on forever. Closing her eyes against the pain, Allie tried to dislodge the tightening rock in her throat.

Dal would not reach out for her, and she had no right to reach for him. Long ago she learned that caring for someone took time and energy, of which she had little now. What affection she had must be carefully husbanded for the daughter she loved.

There was no room in her heart for a hired cowboy.

The next day Allie, leading Jessie by the hand, came upon Dal fashioning a strange contraption. Coils of barbed wire lay in the dirt beside him, along with a dozen old gunny sacks and a jug of compound pesticide solution. He stood in the sun outside the barn, and since the weather had warmed to the low sixties, his shirtsleeves were rolled above his elbows and his shirt was partially unbuttoned. His battered hat had been pushed onto the back of his head while he worked.

Hands protected inside heavy gloves, he twisted four strands of twenty-foot-long pieces of barbed wire lengthwise.

Allie paused beside him and tried to make sense of his project. "I'm afraid to ask," she said good-naturedly. "But I will. What *are* you doing?"

As he answered he continued to twist the wire. "It's a back rubber."

"Mommy has one in the shower!" Jessie squealed. "Hers has a brush on the end."

Dal grinned at the little girl. "You've got the right idea. But that's a back *washer*. Not a back rubber. And it's for a much prettier back." He met Allie's gaze over Jessie's head. In the bright sunlight, his green eyes were alight with humor and warmth and Allie's mind filled with images of Dal washing the length of her bare, sensitive spine....

Fortunately he went on. "This one's for the cattle. Look here, Jessie, and see how I do this. I'm going to tie those gunny sacks around the wire real good, then pour a solution of bug killer over it."

Allie looked at the string of wire and then around the corral. "Then what?"

"I'll take it out to the cattle and string it between gate posts the cattle pass through each day on their way to water."

"And just walking beneath they'll rub the pesticide over their backs every day!" Allie finished in pleased surprise. "It'll save a lot of money not having to spray them—what a great idea!" She knew her smile was glowing.

Dal shrugged, but he was smiling, too. "I can't take complete credit. Lots of ranches use them. But if part of our problem is from ticks, the back rubber will help."

"Oh, this is fantastic!" Allie exclaimed. Yet again Dal was cutting costs—saving her much-needed money with innovative and efficient ideas. She smiled at him brilliantly and barely contained her impulse to throw her arms around his neck.

"We'll still have to spray them once in a while, so it's not a fix-all," he warned. "And I'll have to make several, one for every seventy-five animals or so."

When Jessie tugged free of Allie's hold to play nearby with the kittens, Allie stepped forward, her heart curiously full. She touched Dal's forearm above the glove and felt his warm skin and the springy covering of hair. "Dal, I—I know you don't want me to thank you for anything—and I won't," she added when he would interrupt. "It's just... I..." She trailed off, her eyes threatening to fill with unexpected tears. She wanted to get on her knees and hug his legs like Jessie often did. She wanted to lay her head on his chest and breathe in his earthy scent. She wanted—

"It's all right," Dal replied slowly. "This is a bitch of a job. I've already stuck myself once, despite these gloves." He smiled slowly, his gaze lingering on her mouth. "So, I'll accept thanks for this, okay?"

"Yes," she said breathlessly, her fingers tightening unconsciously on his arm. "I—I wish I could pay you more." Blinking quickly, she made a huge effort to get herself under control. What was the matter with her? She *never* cried!

"There is something you can do for me." He watched her, his hands still on the wire.

"Name it."

In answer, he put the wire aside and pulled the top of his right glove back. A nasty scratch had rent the skin in a two-inch swath. "Doctor this for me, will you?"

"Of course," she replied promptly. "You'll have to come to the house. The first-aid supplies are in the bathroom."

"Yes, ma'am." With a grin he coiled the barb wire and laid it safely on the table, then started for the house with Jessie and Allie.

Installing the four-year-old in front of the television, Allie led the way to her small bathroom. The hallway was dark and narrow, and in the quiet house, with only the low sounds of the television in the other room, oddly intimate.

They passed her bedroom, and she noticed Dal looking inside with interest. He hesitated fractionally in her doorway, taking in the few pieces of inexpensive furniture and lingering on her neatly made bed with its patchwork quilt.

Although she was accustomed to having Dal in her house, it was usually to eat a meal and leave, or to inform her of some ranch business. Today he towered close behind her, his big body almost touching her back as she withdrew disinfectant and bandages from the medicine cabinet over the sink.

She found it terribly annoying that she couldn't seem to inhale deeply enough, her breath coming with a shallowness that had everything to do with Dal's proximity. If only he wouldn't stand so *close!*

All at once she found the room abnormally warm. Without thinking, she stripped off her sweatshirt and gestured roughly for Dal to sit on the edge of the tub. She threw the sweatshirt onto the back of the commode and faced him with the supplies.

He sat, his knees spread, and held his gloves in one hand. With his other he took off his hat and tossed it on top of her sweatshirt. Since there was nowhere for her to sit save on the lowered lid of the commode, she knelt between his knees and set her supplies on the floor. His eyes never left her face.

"Well!" she said brightly. "It's a good thing your sleeve is already rolled up so we don't have to do that."

He raised a brow.

"I'll just apply the disinfectant first and then use these bandages..." She trailed off, realizing she was chattering to fill the silence. Casting around for another subject, she seized on one. "Uh, what will you be doing this afternoon?" It didn't occur to her to *tell* him to do anything anymore. He knew as well or better than she about the ranch's chores.

"Windmill three needs a tail spring. I'll replace it and grease the workings while I'm up there." Dropping his gloves onto the linoleum floor, he reached out and captured the end of the braid that fell over her shoulder. Idly he played with it.

Allie bent over the wound and dabbed it with a soaked cotton swab. On close inspection she could see that her original estimation had been wrong. It wasn't so bad, really, a shallow scratch that hadn't even bled much. Cowboys lived and worked through such injuries routinely without even considering bandaging them.

So why had he suggested she care for it?

Why had she rushed to do so?

His hand rode up her braid, and she was finding it ever more difficult to concentrate on her task. Seldom had she been so close to Dal. Since he'd kissed her that night, they had both been scrupulous about keeping a good physical distance from each other.

But his knees almost embraced her now, and she caught his familiar scent of warm musky male. This near, she could hardly avoid seeing his broad, muscular shoulders, or fail to notice the crisp curling hair that sprang from his open shirt collar. She couldn't help being flustered and unsure by the directness of his intensely observing eyes. With fingers made clumsy by nerves, she quickly cut a small piece of gauze and prepared to tape it on.

"You've got goose bumps," Dal observed almost off-handedly. "Why?" His hand was on her nape now, gently stroking.

"I—I don't know. It's cold in here."

"Then why'd you take off your sweatshirt?"

She met his stare with a level one of her own. "Because."

One side of his mouth kicked up in a faint smile. "That doesn't quite explain it."

Biting off the piece of tape, she smoothed it over the gauze on his hand and began gathering her supplies. "I guess I'm a little nervous, that's all."

"Why?"

"Because I—because you . . ." She got to her knees and clutched everything to her chest. Frowning fiercely, she told him, "I was afraid you might—might grab me and kiss me again."

"I might." At the back of her neck his hand gently urged her toward him.

She resisted. "L-last time you said it was a mistake. You said I should forget it." It was time to get to her feet and walk out of the room. Just walk away.

"I know what I said. Have you been able to forget it? I haven't." Only inches away, his breath fanned her cheeks.

"I don't want to talk about it," she got out, her voice a bare whisper. Her traitorous body was beginning to hum with excitement.

"No?" he replied softly. "I don't want to talk, either. I want to kiss you, Allie. In fact, I want to so badly it's killing me. Every day it's getting worse—my guts are all tied up in knots thinking about you—wanting you. Couldn't you put a poor cowboy out of his misery and just give me one little kiss?"

Allie tried and failed to repress the smile that curved her lips. The idea of Dal as a "poor miserable cowboy" was ludicrous. His words had startled her, thrilled her. And would kissing him be such a terrible thing? After all, he'd asked for nothing and given his all in return. She owed him so much.

That was it—she was grateful to him. The idea made her relax, and she felt a returning confidence suffuse her. Of course that's all she felt for Dal. Gratitude. And if he asked for so little, couldn't she give him that?

"Just a *small* kiss," she answered kindly. Leaning forward, she offered primly closed lips.

"Thank you," he said, more than a hint of laughter in his tone. But first he surprised her by taking the things from her hands and setting them back on the floor. Then he clasped her hands around his neck and smoothly slid his arms around her waist. His big palms went to the vulnerable area of her lower back and pulled her into him.

Before she knew it his lips had taken hers by storm. No gentle, prim gift was he about to take, she realized belatedly.

At first she reacted as she had the first time he'd kissed her: she merely accepted his embrace.

After all, she was bestowing on him a gift, wasn't she? If the kiss was a trifle more…*heated* than she'd bargained for, well, she could adapt.

Yet as Dal's mouth grew more insistent, his hold on her stronger, the answering response in her own body grew apace.

As his tongue forced into her mouth and made sweeping intimate forays, she felt stirrings of alarm. She found she had little defense against him. Crushed to his chest, her breasts bloomed. They grew weighted and heavy, and her nipples tightened with sharp tingles that sent arrows of desire down through her body to pool at the juncture of her thighs.

Allie's eyes flew wide open, then slowly drifted closed.

The tension flowed through her in thick, swollen rivers. Sensing her reaction, Dal tightened his hold, one hand sweeping over her back to clench into her buttocks and guide her flush to his groin. She felt him—felt his hard need demanding acknowledgment. And the answering fire within her burst into flame.

Suddenly she couldn't get enough of him. This was Dal. *Dal*—the man she relied on—the man who cared for her and hers. In feverish need, she thrust her fingers into his hair, finding the texture just as silky soft as she'd imagined. Returning his ardor, she kissed him back with every ounce of her being. It was no time to question her actions or analyze her own fierce need for this mysterious man who'd ridden into her life through all the hot colors of a sunset.

He slipped a hand between their bodies, moving it up her ribs to cup one aching breast. His thumb brushed across her nipple. Over her thin T-shirt and bra, the hard rasp of his calluses lightly abraded her. In his arms she twisted sinuously against him. A low, barely audible moan escaped her lips, and he caught the inflaming sound in his mouth.

Into her mind exploded vivid images of the two of them making passionate love. She saw and felt his big body making her his in the most fundamental way possible. In the grip of the fantasy, she arched closer.

But Dal drew back an inch and pushed her head into his shoulder. He breathed heavily for a moment. "I don't think," he said thickly, "the bathroom floor is the best place for this."

Allie kept her eyes shut, unwilling to release the drugging urgency that gripped her. She drew her lips over his neck, his skin warm and faintly salty. In his strong arms she felt sexy and protected and wonderful. All her worries faded away.

"Honey." He gave her a little shake when she made no reply. Smoothing back the wispy blond hairs that clung to her forehead, Dal forced her to acknowledge him.

"What?" she answered belatedly. The linoleum beneath her knees was getting uncomfortably hard. Lord! Jessie could have wandered in at any moment! Behind his head she could see the cracked tile in the shower that she'd been wanting to regrout. In the living room the noise of the cartoons Jessie watched became audible again.

Still, she was slightly annoyed with Dal. Why had he interrupted the fantastic interlude? "What is it?" she repeated.

"Come on, honey." He continued to stroke her hair. "We can't stay in here all day. There's work to be done. Remember?"

"Work?"

"Yeah. I've gotta go string that back rubber. Pete's coming over after school to help. I thought I'd put him to work making a couple more." He went on, detailing what he hoped to accomplish that day, while Allie slowly came back to the present. The realities of her responsibilities swamped down on her, and she listened with half an ear to the cartoons her daughter watched in the next room.

Frowning, she suspected Dal was going on to give her a chance to recover with dignity. After all, just moments ago she'd been acting like an abandoned hussy!

Smoothing her braid, she disengaged herself and stood, her knees aching a little. In her heart she knew that although Dal was inherently kind, the embraces they shared meant nothing to him. He could kiss her socks off one minute and talk about shoeing a horse the next.

But she couldn't.

She'd had only one lover in her life—and she'd chosen him unwisely. To slide carelessly into bed with Dal went against all the morals of the well-brought-up young girl she'd been. She'd made that mistake once—she wasn't about to make it again!

So her kisses with Dal must be put behind her, she vowed. Or at least put into their proper perspective. They were kisses, nothing more. *Not* a prelude to bed.

Chapter Seven

"**D**ang you, you broom-tail nag!" Pete shouted at the chestnut gelding before him. The horse snorted and bobbed his head. To Allie it appeared as if the curved edges of his mouth almost smiled.

"What's wrong, Pete?" Allie asked, walking toward the corral where Pete stood. But she knew. She'd seen the horse take a small nipping bite at Pete's backside.

He rubbed the offended area. "This crow bait don't know the difference between my backside and a bale of hay."

"Now, Pete," Dal said from where he stood nearby working with another of the recaptured cow ponies they'd brought in. "He's just playin'. Don't be afraid of him."

"Afraid!" Pete squawked, sounding much like one of Allie's hens. "There's only two things I'm afraid of—a decent woman and being left afoot."

Chuckling, Dal said, "Well, I don't know about the woman, but you will be left afoot if you can't learn to get along with that animal. There's always a reason a horse does something. Figure it out." He resumed currying the buckskin's dusty flanks.

Intrigued, Allie climbed onto the corral rails and watched how Pete handled the problem. Jessie was napping, lunch was over; she had a few minutes to spare. The day was bright and sunny and the world looked good. She'd rather be outside, anyway. In the corral, every time Pete turned his back to collect a grooming brush or perform some chore, the chestnut would stretch out his neck and try to clamp his teeth onto Pete's buttocks.

Pete would swear, push the horse away and get more nipping as a reward. "Dog meat, that's all you're good for," Pete muttered, popping the horse lightly on the muzzle. But he merely tossed his head and waited for Pete to turn again.

Allie stifled a giggle.

Taking pity, Dal set aside his brush and walked over to where Pete fumed. He put a fatherly hand on the boy's shoulder and assumed a patient tone. "Why do you suppose a horse would be interested in your tail end, boy?"

"I don't know why," Pete exclaimed heatedly, glaring at the horse. "Because he's a stupid hammerhead, I guess."

"No," Dal explained even more patiently. "You're the stupid hammerhead."

That brought Pete's head around.

Allie smiled, looking at the two males—one slight, young and naive, the other big, fully mature, worldly. Dal exuded the faintest air of danger, Allie decided, comparing them. She was never sure how he'd react to a given situation. She felt a small shiver go up her back.

But Dal was exhibiting patience now. "Son, in order to understand why a horse does something, you've got to think like a horse. Have you got anything in your pockets he might want?"

"No! They're empty."

"Okay. You been sitting on any bales of hay or maybe some sweet feed?"

"No. These jeans are clean."

"Okay. Then we've got to look for another reason. Allie, who used to ride this horse?"

"My father," she replied promptly.

Dal pursed his lips and nodded. "All right. Now, don't get upset when I ask this, 'cause I didn't know your dad. How'd he treat the horse? Ever use a whip or get rough with him?"

"Never. My father was all gentleness with the horses."

"That's good." He turned back and inspected the animal. "He doesn't look mad, anyway. He looks...playful. You can see it in his body language."

"His what?" Pete scratched his head.

"Animals have body language, just like people. You know when a horse is angry, don't you?"

"Well, sure. His ears'll lay back flat and his tail snaps up and down—maybe he'll even show his teeth or raise a hoof to kick."

"See? And how do you know if he's alert and happy?"

"His ears are forward," Pete replied dutifully. "And he's calm—" he cast another glare at the chestnut "—but he isn't trying to bite!"

"Aw, he likes you. He's not trying to hurt you."

"Not trying to hurt! You let him get those big yellow teeth into *your* butt and we'll see—"

"Hey!" Allie jumped down from the rail and hurried toward them. "I remember my dad always carried a red handkerchief in his back pocket. When this horse was a colt, he'd grab the handkerchief whenever Dad would turn his back. It was a game, and they both enjoyed it."

"Well, I'll be darned." Pete scratched his head as Dal chuckled and unknotted a neckerchief from his throat. He stuffed it into Pete's back pocket, leaving a bit to hang out.

Allie climbed back onto the rails and watched Pete resume grooming the animal.

It took five minutes, but suddenly the chestnut swiveled his head around to where Pete stood at his side and neatly lipped the red cloth from the pocket. He bobbed his head, flinging it up and down.

Pete laughed. "Well, maybe we'll save you from the meat factory yet."

Smiling, Allie met Dal's gaze and slowly nodded. It was one reason she was beginning to like him so much. He was so good with the animals, always stopping to figure out the why of their behavior, trying to see the world from their perspective. And with surprising regularity, he *could* figure them out.

Her eyes went to the worn chaise longue mattress hung on the fence. One of the horses he'd brought in, a rangy gray mare, went around rubbing her head on everyone and everything she could find. The problem was habitual. After ruling out pests or the tickle of dried sweat, Dal finally decided to give her something to rub on. The chaise longue mattress served admirably, the mare was happy, and Allie was amazed and delighted when the horse stopped knocking everyone down in her effort to ease the itch.

"We're about ready for roundup," Dal announced, giving his buckskin a last pat. "These seven we brought in are all topped off and lined out—ready to work. It's time to get your cattle marked, Allie. All right if we hire a few men from town to help get the job done?"

"Sure." She'd made sure there was enough money in her dwindling account to pay for roundup. He knew better than she did about the particulars of how many men they'd need and for how long, for which she was grateful. "But I can help, too."

"We'll need your help," Dal agreed, crossing the corral to her side. He looked up at her and put a warm hand on her knee. "But not with the cattle."

"Huh?" The feel of his big hand gently caressing her knee made her uneasy. Instantly memories of their passionate kiss in her house burst into mind. For such a hard-looking mouth, his lips were incredibly soft...like velvet. She could almost feel them pressed to hers now.

"We'll need your help in the kitchen," he was saying. "A roundup crew eats a lot, Allie. Three meals a day is a big job. You're elected." He let his hand slide off her leg and made for the gate.

"B-but I want to help with the branding..."

"Roast beef and gravy is a good choice," he called over his shoulder. "Fried chicken and potatoes. Juicy hamburgers and fries." He disappeared inside the barn, but she could still hear him calling out menus.

Giving in, she smiled and sighed. He was right. She'd be of far more use preparing meals than herding cattle. And this way she wouldn't have to hire a cook. Maybe she could get Tricia to help, though. It would be a full-time job. And probably for the best. The work would allow her little time to moon over the shape and texture of a certain cowboy's mouth.

Within three days she found herself sleepily serving a 5:00 a.m. pot of rich black coffee to more than a half dozen cowboys. Dal outlined his strategy for roundup and gave each man his job. She knew all of them.

They were a good crew, men born and raised in the area and accustomed to ranch work. Dal had chosen well, she decided, setting plates of bacon and eggs and toast before each man.

They were gone before she was fully awake, and she slumped at the table to survey the huge mess of dirty plates and pots. In that instant she decided she would definitely

hire Tricia to help. But she had one memory to keep her
warm.

Somehow Dal had been the last man out the door, and
he'd lingered a moment longer than the others. "Thanks for
the sandwiches." He patted the saddlebags full of food.
"We'll be gone all day, getting a bunch closer in for branding. What will you do while we're gone?"

She raised a brow. He'd never asked that before. With a
baleful glance around the messy kitchen and thoughts of the
big dinner she'd have to cook, in addition to all her other
daily chores, she shrugged. "I imagine I'll keep busy."

He chuckled and started out the door. "That's my girl."

"I'm not a girl," she said without thinking.

In one slow, sweeping glance, he took in her small, com-
pact body outlined in black cotton leggings and a blue-
checked Western shirt, the tails of which she'd knotted at
her waist. "No, honey, I know that. But it's easier for me if
I don't think too much about the womanly parts of you. If
I did that, I'd never get any work done at all." Slinging the
saddlebags onto his shoulder, he tugged his hat low over his
eyes and leaned down to press a hard kiss on her mouth.
Before she could open her eyes, the screen door banged shut
behind him.

From her vantage at the window, Allie found herself
craning her neck as far as she could in order to see him ride
out. Even though he couldn't know if she watched or not,
he waved at the house.

And even though she knew he couldn't possibly see her,
she waved back.

Dal was indispensable, and Allie lived in fear he'd realize
just how much she counted on him. With the help of the
extra men, they got the first bunch of cattle moved in close
to the ranch and started branding in the big pens. The calves
were separated from their mothers, inoculated against dis-

ease and branded. The cows had their hooves trimmed and were ear-tagged for more efficient management, Dal explained to Allie. Ear-tagging was something her father had never bothered with, but which Dal considered important.

One man was assigned the job of tallying each cow and her calf by writing all pertinent information about them into a ledger and corresponding it to the number in the cow's ear. Each step along the way he explained to Allie, although she already knew most of it. After two days of Dal's patient, thorough explanations, she began to get the impression that he was educating her for a reason.

Trying to keep the suspicion out of her voice, she asked him, "Why are you explaining all this to me, Dal?"

He looked surprised. "Because it's your ranch. You ought to know how to run it."

"But you're here."

"That's right, I'm here now." He took off his hat and fanned his face.

Left unsaid, she knew, was his earlier warning: *I'll work for you, boss lady, but only for a time. The minute you start relying on me, I'll be gone.*

Heart sinking, Allie realized she'd been hoping he would stay on indefinitely. She wanted to ask how long he would remain. She wanted to ask why he ever had to go, but she'd learned from experience he didn't like being pressed.

With an effort she summoned a smile. "Well, the work is going well, isn't it?"

"Nobody's gotten kicked yet. Or gored. Nobody's gotten thrown off his horse or stomped by a freshly castrated steer. So, I guess, yeah, the work's going well." He grinned and set his hat back on at a jaunty angle.

"That's not what I meant and you know it." She pretended to punch him in the arm. "I mean the cattle are mostly healthy, and there seems to be more than I'd originally thought. We should have a good sale day in the fall."

"We'll know better about the numbers at the end of roundup. It's gonna take several more days yet." He put a hand on her shoulder and squeezed. "But, you're right. We might just break even come shipping day."

She laughed lightly, knowing this was good news. To break even on a cattle ranch was good. Making a profit was tremendous. Putting her hand atop his, she rubbed her fingers over his knuckles. "Thanks, Dal. You're good."

His grin widened and she knew he remembered what Jessie had said to him after he'd bandaged her hen-pecked hand. Gruffly he asked, "Think so?"

She nodded, still smiling up at him. In a tiny shock she realized he was looking at her mouth.

"Maybe," he suggested slowly, "you owe me a little something, then."

"I'm paying you fair wages."

His arched brow said more than any words.

"Okay," she relented. "Maybe not quite as much as you're worth. What did you have . . . in mind?" It was embarrassing, how breathless her voice had gotten all of a sudden.

"Dal!" One of the hands called over to him. "You gonna stand around all day? I could use some help with the inoculatin' gun."

"Be right there," Dal called back. To Allie he said, "I'll leave the manner of my payment to you."

"I—I'll bake you a chocolate cake," she said as he moved away.

"That's a good start, honey. Keep thinking on it, though. You'll get it."

She pretended puzzlement. "Two chocolate cakes?"

His hoot of laughter floated back to her over the loud bawl of the cattle, and she headed up to the house with a small smile on her face. It was obvious he wanted another kiss, and the knowledge thrilled her. It also scared her to death. After the last time, she wasn't sure she could keep her head. It was odd, she reflected, slowly climbing the steps, that it wasn't the man she couldn't trust, but herself.

With Tricia's help, Allie cooked and cleaned and did everything she could to help the hard-working men do their job. Whenever she got the chance, she took Jessie out to the pens to watch the progress and silently thank Dal for his knowledge and his drive. What *was* driving him, she didn't know, but he worked as hard as two men.

Black Jack, his enormous gelding, was the envy of every cowhand. A beautiful quarter horse, he stood a full seventeen hands, had a finely arched neck and an ebony coat unrelieved by white. It gleamed with vitality in the heat of the spring sun. Allie knew he was Dal's pride and joy.

She watched Dal urge him now after a particularly recalcitrant calf. Black Jack's heavily muscled haunches gathered and catapulted him forward. Overhead, Dal's lariat whirled, shot out and slipped over the calf's head. Automatically the well-trained horse backed up, keeping the line taut while another rider "heeled" the calf, throwing him.

The gelding stood his ground, ears either straight forward or flicking back to catch Dal's quiet commands.

"What'll you take for that gelding?" Josh Barnett, a wiry man in his forties asked Dal suddenly from across the branding pen. "I'd give a lot to own him."

Grinning, Dal patted the animal's neck and shook his head. "You don't have enough money, Josh."

Hoisting Jessie on top of the corral fence, Allie sat beside her and listened to the goings-on. Another of the hands glanced up, a branding iron steaming in his hand. "Maybe I do. If you're thinking of letting him go, I'd like a chance to bid on him."

Two of the others looked up eagerly.

"Sorry," Dal said. "I'm attached to the cayuse. Raised him up from a colt, trained him myself. He enjoys his work too much to ever let go."

Pete stamped to his feet, allowing a recently branded calf to lumber onto four legs. He dusted off his hands and boasted, "Dal's right. That horse'll run a cow down a prairie dog hole and paw the ground till she comes out."

The men laughed and even Jessie giggled. Dal dismounted and came over, wiping sweat from his forehead with his arm, and tweaked one of her long braids. "When you get your pinto pony, miss, I'll help you train him, okay?"

"Okay," she answered promptly. "But I don't want him running down any doggie holes."

"It's a deal."

"Dal," Allie interjected, "we don't know exactly when Jess will be able to get her pony. It could be a long way off." She looked at him hard, warning him against raising her daughter's hopes.

"Maybe so. Maybe not," the uncooperative man said. "But he'll be a good one, eh, Jess?"

"Right." The girl shifted her small bottom on the rough rail and asked Dal a few silly questions. He answered them patiently while Allie tried not to worry. Why did the man have to lead the girl on so?

Jessie wanted down to play with her kittens, and Dal carefully lifted her, cautioning her to stay far back from the corral. When she skipped off, he turned to Allie. "I've made up my mind to see that Jess has her pony soon. I'll buy him myself."

Allie almost snorted. She knew he had no money, and the subsistence pay she was able to give him could hardly buy a horse. Besides, it wasn't his responsibility. She told him so.

"I'm making it my responsibility," he shot back. "And I'll teach her to ride him, too." His expression was grimly challenging; he looked like a man ready to do battle over a range war, instead of merely acquiring a mount for one four-year-old girl.

Allie felt like laughing and crying all at once. Even though Slade had said essentially the same thing, Allie didn't feel the same about the offer. She knew Dal meant it from his heart, and it touched her he was willing to fight her over this matter.

Did this change their situation? Would he ever consider staying on...permanently? Was she actually stupid enough to fall for a man like Dal—a *criminal?* The man had a shady past and he admitted it. He wouldn't be the kind of man she'd told him she wanted—a steady, stable worker. No, he was just a drifter.

Allie searched his eyes and tried to read his thoughts. Perspiration dripped freely down his lean cheeks, and his hat was stained dark with sweat. Even the front of his faded green work shirt was damp. Such exertion...and all for her.

His eyes glittered as they met hers, gradually taking on a hungry gleam. Lowering his voice, he asked, "You give any thought to how you're gonna pay your debt to me?"

"What debt?" she asked, widening her eyes innocently. "You ate three pieces of my chocolate cake. We're quits."

"I'll tell you when we're quits, and it's not yet. I'll be collecting my full payment. Tonight."

"Tonight?" Before he could react, she slipped through the rails and started backing toward the house, unable to withhold a smile. "But I have so much to do. I'm very busy. There's the cooking and cleaning. I'm afraid I won't have a spare moment for you, Dal."

Holding her palms up, she took two more steps back and saw that he was grinning. In spite of her deep misgivings she liked flirting with Dal. "As a matter of fact, I'll be busy all week. Perhaps I could bake for you, say... next week? Another chocolate cake *is* what you want, isn't it? I'll have to get the ingredients.''

He draped both arms over the top rail and called softly, "You run around getting ingredients and keepin' busy all you want, honey. But it won't save you from me. I'll run you to ground when it's time.''

Amazingly, Allie blushed. Instead of a fully mature twenty-four-year-old woman, and a mother to boot, she felt an awkward fourteen. Chastizing herself for her ridiculous reaction, she averted her face and mounted the steps in a hurry, escaping into the house. Dal's soft, good-natured laughter followed her all the way into the kitchen.

Dinner was a raucous affair, with eight hungry men clumping into her small house in heavy boots amid loud teasing and laughter. Quickly, Allie and Tricia served them, placing in front of each man brimming plates of sliced ham, scalloped potatoes and vegetables. There were ice-cold cans of beer, milk and sodas, and for dessert three apple pies Tricia had made from scratch.

Pushing back from the table with a satisfied pat on his rounded stomach, Josh smiled at the eighteen-year-old. "That shore was good pie, Miz Tricia. I was hungry enough to eat a saddle blanket.''

"And you would, too,'' another ribbed him. "But he's right. The pie is great.''

"Well, thank you,'' Tricia said primly, removing plates. "It's nice to be appreciated. My mama taught me how to make a flaky crust years ago, and it's not easy, let me tell you.''

Pete smiled gently as she stopped at his shoulder. "You learn well, Trish. The pie was delicious.''

Pursing her lips, Tricia shrugged as if Pete's compliment meant nothing. She snatched his plate of half-eaten pie away to the sink.

"Hey," he yelped, "I'm not finished."

"Yes, you are." She stacked dirty dishes on top of his pie, squishing it down. "I can't be hanging around forever waiting for you cowboys to finish. I've got to get home. I've got a date tonight."

Immediately Pete's expression darkened. "With who? It's not Slade Hunt, is it?" At that, Dal's head jerked up sharply.

"None of your business." She turned on the water faucet full blast and began washing.

Allie edged toward Pete and used her sponge on the table to wipe up crumbs. Leaning close, she whispered, "It's just her dad. He's taking her to see a movie."

"Oh." His gaze went to the girl busily rinsing glasses. Slowly he smiled and leaned his chair onto its back two legs. "I'll be going out tonight, too," he announced in a voice loud enough to carry over the rushing water. "Thought I'd take in a movie."

A soapy washcloth in her hand, Tricia glared over her shoulder at Pete. There were only a few movie theaters in town. Chances were they'd see each other.

Beneath the table Allie kicked him in the shin. She whispered, "I only told you that so you wouldn't be jealous. Stop teasing her, will you?"

"Sorry," he whispered back. "Can't." In a louder voice he casually said to Tricia, "Maybe we'll run into each other in town. Then I'll get a chance to see who this mystery date of yours is."

Josh, who'd been following the exchange, snickered. Allie kicked him, too, and when he howled, she pretended ignorance. Fortunately the others were caught up in a conversation about a crazy cow that had gotten turned around in the chute and in her panic nearly broke down the ancient wooden rails.

To Pete, Allie said, "Honestly, you're getting more like
Dal every day. Stubborn and ornery and full of the devil. I
think he's been a poor influence on you." She threw a mock
glare at Dal.

"I don't know about Dal's influence." Tricia placed two
dripping fists on her hips. "But Pete is stubborn and ornery."

The accused one leaned farther back in his chair and laced
his fingers together over his flat belly. A supremely satisfied smile stretched Pete's mouth wide. He knew he'd gotten Tricia's goat, and it was obvious. He'd see her in town
with her "date" and it would be her father. She'd never live
it down.

Taking in Pete's smug expression, Tricia whirled and began banging pots and pans around. Dal leaned close to Pete.
"Have some sympathy, boy. Same as you, she's just trying
to grow up. She's got her pride, don't strip it from her.
Eventually she'll see the value in a man who respects that."

Even as Dal spoke, Pete's smile faded. "Guess you're
right. I am pretty tired. Maybe I'll turn in early so I can get
an early start in the morning."

Dal smiled his approval, and Allie smiled at Dal. He was
such a sensitive man, so caring. He understood that people
needed to save face, keep up pretenses, hold on to a bit of
vanity. In that moment she knew she'd give Dal his kiss,
whenever he wanted it, however he wanted it. Knowing she
was misty-eyed and completely unable to help it, she gazed
at him and smiled tremulously. She was crazy about the
man.

Belatedly he caught the look and blinked. His brows rose
and he appeared stunned by the brilliance of her expression. She held his eyes and knew she was leading him on and
didn't care. Dal *was* good.

She knew he'd hang around after all the others, including Tricia, had left. She knew he'd collect his kiss.

Because the nights were still chilly, he built a roaring fire for Allie in her stone fireplace, and Jessie curled up on a nest of blankets before it. In minutes the girl was fast asleep. With the kitchen cleaned and the work finished for the day, Allie sighed and sat on the carpeted floor a few feet away from her daughter. Her eyes went to the leaping flames, and the mesmerizing play of light soothed her.

Without invitation Dal sat in the big vinyl easy chair behind her and drew her back to lean against his knee. She could feel him toying with her long braid and closed her eyes. A small peace stole over her. She was home, watching the child she loved sleeping, the sweet curve of the girl's cheek peachy in the firelight. And touching her with gentle, reverent fingers was the man who was beginning to rustle a corner of her heart.

Why not relax? The cattle work was going well. Dal had made no definitive statement about leaving, and for the first time she truly believed the ranch might make it. Turning slightly, she leaned back between Dal's legs and rubbed her cheek against his knee. She knew she owed him everything.

In the silence of the room she could hear his heavy swallow, and she was aware he watched her. When her hair spread about her shoulders and fell straight and thick to her hips, she realized he'd removed the band and unbraided it. She sat up in surprise.

"Where's your brush, Allie?" he asked softly.

"What?" Never in her life had anyone but her or her mother brushed her hair. Certainly no man.

"Well, it's in the bathroom." She twisted to face him. He didn't mean he was actually going to—

"Go get it." His voice was low, gentle, commanding.

She rose automatically. "I'll put Jess to bed." Lifting the sleeping girl in her arms, she carried her to her bedroom and tucked her beneath the covers. In a moment she was back. When she hesitated before him, he tugged her onto the floor between his legs again. With the first soft glide of the bristles on her sensitive scalp and the pull all the way through to the end of the golden strands, she sighed in pleasure.

Ever since she'd left home, years ago, to stupidly run off with Paxton, she'd had no one to pamper her, no one to sacrifice for her, give to her, see to her wishes or want to please her. It was so long since anyone had cared for her. But Dal did now. She could feel his affection and tenderness in every stroke of the brush and in the comforting brace of his strong thighs. It was in everything he did on the ranch. Surely this wasn't a man who could simply up and leave her on a whim. By the day, she became more certain that this place was growing on him.

"Your hair is like my sister's," he told her quietly. "Only hers is dark brown, almost black. But it's thick and long, too. I . . . miss her."

"Tell me about your sister," she whispered.

He chuckled, but she could see the wistfulness in him. "You'd like her. She's a spitfire, like you. Fights for everything, and because she was the youngest and I'm the oldest, I had a definite big-brother attitude about her."

"Did you vet all her dates when she got old enough?" Allie could imagine the "big brother" throwing one of the swains out on his ear for the slightest transgression.

His chuckle deepened. "Her boyfriends had to go through me and my two younger brothers. And we were pretty tough judges, as I recall."

"How'd she ever get a date with you three overprotective gorillas hanging around?"

Pausing a moment to rub his chin, Dal shook his head, and his smile grew rueful. "I don't recall any guy ever meeting all of our requirements."

Allie's eyes widened. "She never got any dates at all because of you?"

He shrugged. "For a time. When she hit about sixteen or seventeen, she was darn tired of our interference and started meeting her boyfriends at the local burger joints and teenage hangouts."

"And...did she ever marry?"

Shocking her, Dal's hands fell away from her hair and she turned to see a bleakness settle over his features. His jaw tightened, worked, and his eyes turned inward with some remembered agony. He missed his family terribly, she could see that. But there was something else, some other pain that ate at him.

"Dal?"

"Hmm?" He still wasn't with her, she could tell.

"Dal," she repeated, "it's all right. You don't have to talk about it anymore. Just...brush my hair, won't you?" Turning her back, she presented him with the task, hoping to get his mind off whatever had triggered the painful memory. Maybe his sister had contracted a terrible disease and died. But he talked about her in the present tense. She couldn't be dead. What else could it be? Allie could only guess. But it wasn't in her anymore to push for answers just to satisfy her curiosity. All she wanted for him now was a return to serenity.

For long moments she stared into the flames of the fire, watching the tongues leap and play in beautiful sunset shades of orange and red and yellow. After a bit Dal resumed brushing. He said nothing, but she could tell by the careful touch of his hands in her hair that he was coming back to her.

Exactly when his hands left her hair and curved over her shoulders, she wasn't sure. With the play of firelights on the walls of her small living room, the sounds of Dal's deep breathing and the warmth and protectiveness of his big hands soothing her shoulders she calmed to the point of drowsiness.

"So pretty," he breathed in her ear. He let her hair slide through his fingertips. "It's the color of a summer wheatfield." Lifting a bit to his nostrils, he inhaled deeply, then buried his face into her neck. "And you smell like summer, Allie. Like fresh breezes and little flowers."

At the pressure of his palm under her chin, she tilted her head toward him. He was bending close from his seat on the chair, his straddled legs enclosing her, his breath fanning her cheeks. She'd never felt so completely at ease in her life.

When Dal's lips glided over hers with the feather-light touch of a bird's wing, she sighed.

"Come here, honey," he whispered against her mouth as his hands went beneath her arms to lift her. "Sit in my lap awhile. Let me hold you."

Allowing him to pull her up, she found herself in a delicate sprawl across his big body. He reclined the chair so that she lay almost completely atop him, her breast to his, her head tucked beneath his chin. His arms surrounded her and held her captive. As if she wanted to escape!

Allie snuggled closer, loving the feel of his big hands caressing her back in long strokes from her shoulder blades down to just above the curve of her derriere. Growing warmer by the minute, she shifted her weight and pressed her lips to his throat.

"You'd better stop wiggling around like that, Allie, unless you plan to start something you might not want to finish."

"I'm not wiggling," she said, fascinated by the rough texture of his neck where his beard was starting to grow. With her lips, she nibbled along the strong column of his throat, delighting in his quickly indrawn breath. Daringly she worked her way up to his ear and very carefully, very gently, closed her teeth over his lobe.

Dal groaned and his hands stopped in their stroking to clench her buttocks. With a small movement of his hands, he rubbed her over his groin. "Don't pretend you don't know what you're doing to me, Allie. I'm near exhausted tonight, and it's the reason I've been able to get even this close to you. But I'm alive, and I'm a healthy man. Not a saint."

Slowly she drew back to look him fully in the face. Sadly she let her gaze wander over the handsome planes of his masculine jaw and nose, ending with his pale green eyes. "I'm sorry. I wasn't thinking. I don't mean to lead you on, but you're... you're hard to resist, you know. I've been alone such a long time, and you pay such flattering attention to me. I—I guess I've been a little starved for male companionship."

Abruptly Dal's face tightened. "You mean just any man would do? My God, Allie—"

"No." She put two fingers over his mouth. "No. You're the only man I'd allow these liberties. You're the only one I want, Dal." With one last wistful glance, she began to pull away.

His arms closed around her convulsively. "Don't go. Just let me hold you awhile longer... kiss you a little. Please?"

From such a strong man his plea was oddly compelling. She made no move to stop him when he drew her to his mouth and kissed her. She couldn't. At that moment Dal was her world, she admitted to herself shakily. She'd trust him with her life.

The kiss deepened, and Allie responded fully, accepting his tongue into her mouth, putting her hands into his hair and caressing the back of his neck. A sound escaped his lips, something between a groan of satisfaction and a male sigh of pleasure.

Her body, already relaxed, grew tingly and warmer still. Beginning in the nether region of her lower belly, fingers of liquid heat snaked through her veins, pooling in her breasts and causing them to grow heavy and painfully full.

Suddenly the amount of clothing between them became unbearable.

It was with great relief she felt Dal's hand smooth up the front of her crimson blouse and begin to unfasten the mother-of-pearl snaps. His hand slid inside, cupping her breast over her inexpensive cotton bra, and Allie nearly groaned at the exciting sensation. She could feel his calluses even through the cotton fabric as he drew his thumb over one peaked tip.

He moved her slightly, so that she lay cradled across his lap in a manner that allowed him to look at her freely. Giving her a small smile, he unlatched the front catch of her bra and her breasts spilled free. He gasped and she watched through lowered lids as his black pupils dilated and in them danced the flames of the fire.

He seemed unable to draw an ordinary breath, hauling in lungfuls of oxygen while merely looking at her. She glanced down, then, and saw that her breasts, generous for a woman of her size, were proudly displayed and rosy in the dim lighting. Her nipples were achingly taut, beckoning, and as she watched, his hand closed over first one, then the other.

So right, she heard a voice whisper in her mind. The sun-darkened hue of his hand against the pale ivory of her skin looked perfectly natural and as right as the season's change. He was winter, she summer.

She closed her eyes and let her head lean back against his chest. Her hair fell over his arm, tangling over them both. ''Dal,'' she whispered, not knowing what she wanted to say, hardly realizing she was speaking. ''Oh, Dal...''

''Don't be alarmed,'' he warned her softly, ''but I've got to taste you. I have to know what you feel like against my mouth.'' Swiftly he bent to take one crest into his mouth.

Allie gasped and moaned sharply.

"Shh, honey," he crooned against her soft skin. "It's all right. I know what you want. I want it, too."

Against her breast his lips were as she remembered, soft and velvety smooth. But the skin surrounding his mouth hadn't been shaved since before dawn, and the whiskers lightly abraded her nipple, arousing her to a new pitch.

She should call a halt, she really should, a small, weak voice whispered in her ear. She ignored it. She didn't want him to stop. Ever. The blood raced through her veins; her heart thudded so loud she could hear nothing else. She made no move at all to stop him when his hand strayed to her belt buckle. He mumbled something against her breast and she strained to hear.

"What, Dal?" she whispered. It seemed imperative she understand his words.

"So sweet," he muttered. "So giving. I won't survive it. I don't know how I'll live without you."

Beneath his lips, Allie stilled. Her buckle was unfastened now and his hand was sliding beneath the waistband of her jeans. "What...what did you say?"

"I don't think I've ever felt this way about a woman. I'll miss you...so much." He smiled tightly, the glitter of male hunger alive in his eyes.

Pushing his head away, she struggled to sit up an inch. A mild panic doused some of the heat singing through her. "What do you mean, you'll miss me? Are you leaving?"

"Not tonight." His gaze on her breasts was rapt. "If a herd of stampeding steers came through your living room right now, I wouldn't move." Bending toward her breast, he made to take the peak into his mouth again.

With both hands she grabbed his wrist, pushing it away from her jeans. Her fear escalated another notch. "But you have plans to go? When?"

He blinked, then lowered his eyes as if he didn't want to reply.

"You owe me an answer," Allie demanded, her voice rising. She sat up more fully now, put her palms on his shoulders and gripped with her fingers. "Tell me the truth. Will you abandon me, too?"

Chapter Eight

"Abandon?" Dal allowed Allie to sit up straight in his lap but he frowned at her. "Don't you think that's a little strong? I'll be moving on, that's all. I've made it clear enough I would, eventually, so don't pretend otherwise." He hated the way his words came out, so brusque and uncaring. But, dammit, the woman acted as if he'd promised her the world, for God's sake. And right now it was hard to think. The blood was rushing to the center of his body, heating him hotter than a branding fire.

With regret, he watched while Allie yanked together the edges of her blouse, fingers shaking, and began buttoning it. "Yes, of course, I should have remembered. You did say, more than once, you'd be *moving on,* didn't you, Dal? How could such a thing escape me?" Her face was now flushed with anger. She made as if to get off his lap.

Putting an arm across her middle, he asked, "So why are you upset?"

She looked up at the ceiling and pretended to think about that. "Oh, I don't know. Maybe I don't like the idea of being used, that's all. Just a small thing, really."

"*Used!*" A bit of cool clarity came to wash away some of the heat. "Lady, you've got it backward. If anyone around this ranch is getting used it's *me!*" When she went to get off his lap this time, he didn't protest.

Standing before him, she put her hands on her hips. Her hair spread about her shoulders in a wild tangle, and her frown was fierce. "I haven't asked you to do anything you didn't want to." Her words poured forth, as if withheld too long behind a faulty dam. "And—and what's wrong with you? I feel like I have to walk on eggshells all the time, in case I might say something about your past you won't like. No one's allowed to question you, but why? Because you're afraid someone might actually get to know you? Someone might actually begin to *care* about you?"

He got to his feet, his hands balling into fists at his sides. Coming to mind was his sister's horrified screaming, his father's shocked features. Images of blood and death and shame.

But he could tell her none of this. So he said nothing. After a moment a stunned expression crossed over Allie's features.

"That's it, isn't it, Dal? There's something in you that doesn't want anyone to get close because then you'd be vulnerable. If I cared about you...then you might have to care about me!"

"Your logic is flawed," he spat out, crossing to the fireplace and gripping the cold rock mantel in tight fingers. There was little he could say without revealing the whole gruesome truth.

"Is it?" She eyed him angrily, speculation in her face. "Dal takes care of Dal, and that's all, right? A solitary man, aren't you? A drifter. No ties that bind, no shackles—"

"That's enough," he cut in gruffly. "I've taken care of your ranch—and you—while I've been here."

"Sure, you have," she surprised him by agreeing. "But what about after you go? Will you take up with another poor woman rancher trying to raise an illegitimate child?"

His head swung around sharply.

"Yes," she informed him stiffly. "Jessie's illegitimate. Her father didn't hang around long enough to keep his promise to marry me. I…lied to you before. It doesn't matter, though. You'll be leaving. You'll forget me." Her lip quivered and her big blue eyes filled.

In that moment she looked more like a little girl than Jessie. Inside his chest his heart contracted. He took a step toward her, hand outstretched. "Allie, I—"

"Don't." She shrank back. "I'm just glad things didn't get out of hand between us tonight. I would have hated myself in the morning—letting my body get used by a careless cowboy. Unfortunately I've made that mistake before."

"Used!" he shouted, his temper suddenly fraying. "Why do you keep saying that word? I figured we wanted each other—maybe could share a mutually fulfilling experience—"

"Lord, you've quite a vocabulary for a simple working man." Her eyes narrowed. "You're not uneducated, are you? And you don't come from poverty." She drew her hair over one shoulder and began braiding it with quick flicks of her fingers. "You said my hair is like your sister's. Well, I've noticed that every time your family is mentioned, you clam up. What is it with them? Does this *killing* you're supposed to have committed have something to do with them?"

"*Allie.*" His voice was low and full of warning.

"What, Dal?" She used a falsely sweet tone and adopted a patient posture. In the weeks he'd lived on her ranch, he knew she had tried withholding her questions. Yet her expression now was brittle, as if some wall of reserve had burst. The woman didn't know what she was getting into.

"Leave it lie." He turned away and stalked to the hat tree to yank on his coat.

"You're running away already?"

"Yes. All the way to the bunkhouse. A man needs some privacy." He gave her a hard glare and opened the door.

She was there before he could get out, grabbing his arm. "Fine. Leave the ranch, then, when you're ready. But when you go, do yourself a favor—head for your home, wherever it is. Make peace there."

That stung. How could she have guessed and gotten so close to the truth? He tried to shake off her hand, but she held on like a pair of leather hobbles. He said, "You don't know anything about it."

"Yes, I do." When he would protest, she went on. "I don't understand your situation, that's true. But I do know about being estranged from family, from those you love. It happened to me, I allowed it, and it was wrong. Now my parents are gone and I'll never get the chance to make amends."

Something in her speech distracted him. With a measuring glance, he studied her. A cool night breeze intruded from the opened doorway, but he turned away from it. "Is that why you're so darn determined to save this place, Allie? A way to make up to your parents?"

For a moment she didn't respond. Then, when she did answer, her reply was so soft he almost couldn't hear it. "Yes," she whispered. "Oh, God. Yes." Averting her face, she crossed her arms, hugging herself against the invading wind. She wandered back to the fireplace and stopped there, staring down into the flames.

Even as he let himself out, regret dragged at his steps. He wanted to talk to her, explain. But there was so much pain in what he'd done—such hurtful truth. And there was no guarantee she'd understand. A warm, giving woman like Allie—she'd probably recoil from him once she knew. He kicked open the bunkhouse door, went in and slammed it shut. He wouldn't chance it. It would be better to leave, start anew as he'd done so many times. But could he? Could he really *abandon* her, as she put it?

On her knees the next morning in what was left of her mother's rose garden, Allie was determined to bring the blooms back to life. Since the men were all out on the range, she figured she had a good two hours free before they were back, looking for lunch, and that was a beef stew already simmering. Jessie slept peacefully inside.

Allie hoed in the sun for almost an hour, pulled weeds and began trimming off suckers and dead stalks. Beside her was a can of three-way rose food and a bottle of fungus spray.

Leaning on the hoe, she stretched her stiff back and studied the barn across the driveway. Holes in the roof, peeling paint, dry rot—she hated its weathered, unkempt appearance. Once she'd mentioned in passing that she'd like to see it freshly painted. Dal had looked at her with almost comical blankness. "I'm not a painter," he'd said before walking away. Well, she wasn't, either, but as soon as she could afford it, she was going into Lubbock and invest in gallons of the best barn paint she could find—and then tackle the job herself!

It was a simple fact that the work Dal performed, and his efficient management of Pete's time, was beginning to allow Allie to accomplish more. Like the rose work, she reminded herself, tossing away the hoe and collecting the clippers. In the whole past year that she'd struggled here, she had never felt as if her other, more important chores were caught up enough to afford her time for smaller jobs. Because of Dal alone, now she could.

Allie started humming. Even though their terrible argument of the night before had upset her, with the coming of the morning's sun, she'd rallied. Dal would go, she would have to accept that, but if she didn't push him, possibly it wouldn't be so soon. Perhaps he'd stay through the winter. Maybe, if she backed off, he'd even change his mind altogether.

Tricia drove up, getting out of her car wearing hot-pink pumps and matching jeans so tight she appeared spooned into them. She hobbled to Allie through the gravel driveway and observed the work. "Wow," she exclaimed, touching one trimmed stalk with the tip of her finger. "You're really going to town in that rose patch. What color blooms does this one get?"

Allie opened her mouth to answer, but suddenly realized she couldn't remember. She hadn't been home for four years, and when she'd finally returned, the rose patch was half-dead. It saddened her, somehow, that she couldn't recall the colors of her mother's pride and joy.

Saving her a reply, Pete rode up to the house on the chestnut gelding that had given him trouble before. But Pete made sure now to always keep a handkerchief in his back pocket, and man and horse had become fast friends.

As usual, a big smile split Pete's face, but he wasn't looking at Allie. He was looking at Tricia. "Hi," he said to her softly.

"Hi, yourself," she returned, hunching a shoulder away from him. "Allie, have you started supper or should I see about it?"

"It's on the stove," Allie said, stripping off her gloves. "If you'll just thaw some bread loaves and toss a salad, we'll be ready." She turned to Pete. "What are you doing back so soon? I thought I'd get at least another hour's time."

He dismounted and tied his gelding to the gate. "I, ah, forgot something in the barn." His manner was evasive, and he was still looking at Tricia. He'd known she would be arriving about now.

"Is that right?" Allie tried to hide a grin. "What was it?"

"Huh?" He stared at the pretty red curls that fell to Tricia's shoulders as if he'd been hit on the head by a flying horseshoe.

"What did you want," Allie repeated slowly, "in the *barn?*"

"Oh, I don't know." His eyes went to the creamy freckled skin of the girl's face and lingered there. "Just a . . . a rope! Yeah, that's it. Mine broke when I was trying to catch a big steer."

Tricia raised one brow. "You sure your *big* steer wasn't really a *little* calf that didn't break your rope, but instead ran off with it?"

Allie choked to cover her chuckle. She knew that for a cowboy to lose his best rope on a runaway steer or calf was mortifying.

But Pete wasn't offended. If anything, his grin widened. He nudged his hat back, then hung his thumbs on his belt loops. "I've learned a lot from Dal, including how to rope. If I really want to snag a heifer in my loop, she couldn't get away. Not no-how." His blue eyes traveled the length of Tricia's pink jeans, as if to imply *she* was the heifer in question.

Amazing Allie, Tricia flushed. But before Pete could enjoy his victory, Tricia's eyes lifted to the sky-blue truck barreling up the drive. She appeared to forget all about Pete as she hurried to smooth her hair.

For a moment Allie wasn't sure if she was glad to see Slade or not.

Motives, she mused, *were everything.* What could truly be motivating her handsome neighbor's attention to her? Should she be flattered . . . or wary?

With understandable caution, she set aside her gardening tools and prepared to greet him properly. "Hello, neighbor," she said, coming forward. "It's almost hot today, isn't it? How about a cold drink?"

From his truck Slade approached, ignoring the others. Making her uncomfortable, he said nothing for long moments, then stopped a mere four inches away. "A man doesn't need anything else when he's got you to look at, darlin'. You're a treat to the eyes."

"Well, uh—" she flicked an embarrassed glance at Pete and Tricia "—thanks."

He tucked a bit of her hair behind her ear. Without appearing to recoil, she swiftly bent and gathered the tools she'd just set aside, getting out of reach. "What can I do for you?"

"Thought maybe I could do something for you," he drawled, and Allie almost flinched at the innuendo. He chuckled and took a wicked-looking hand rake from her, stroking the metal handle. "I heard you hired some boys from town to help with your gathering and branding."

Pete came down one step, his grin wiped away. Allie knew he held no love for Slade. "That's right."

Slade ignored him. "I told you I'd send my men over for that job. You shouldn't have to be worrying about the extra wages. You know I want to help you, Allie."

Pete came down the last step and glared at Slade. There was a very adult, very masculine set to his shoulders. "We can handle it."

"Thank you for the offer, Slade." Allie edged around so that her body was between Pete and Slade. She didn't want any confrontations between the teenager and the older, stronger man. Pete could get hurt. Bad. Slade's barroom brawls were legion. "We'll call if we need help."

Suddenly Slade frowned at her tools. "Say, what are you doing, anyway—grubbing around in the dirt? Haven't you got a hired man for this maintenance stuff?"

"I like working with the soil," she defended. "And this was once a beautiful rose garden." Wistful, she looked around. "I just realized I can't remember what color each bush produces."

He surveyed the small plot with a bored glance. "Does it matter?"

She shrugged, chagrined. "Well, no. Not really." It didn't matter...except to her. All at once it struck her that Dal wouldn't have been so insensitive. He would have understood.

She watched Slade lip a cigarette from a soft pack and curl his hands around a match.

"I didn't know you still smoked," Allie remarked. "I thought you'd kicked the habit."

He grinned, dragging deeply. "Yeah, well, I alternately kick it and it kicks me back."

"Oh..." Allie shrugged as a small silence drew out. "I'd best get to work." She had little to say to him, anyway, and she still felt uneasy around him. Did he covet her land? Or just her body? She still had no answer.

"All right. I'd best get to work, too." Slade hauled in cigarette smoke and pivoted away.

"Gosh, Slade." Tricia struggled down the steps in her pumps. "You don't have to leave yet, do you? How about staying for lunch? It's stew and fresh-baked bread."

With an arched brow, Allie glanced at Tricia, surprised the girl would take the liberty of inviting her neighbor.

For the first time Slade fully faced Tricia. Through a dissipating cloud of exhaled smoke, he gave her a thorough examination. From her ridiculous pumps to the top of her auburn head, he let his gaze leisurely travel her frame.

When the girl blushed painfully, Allie felt sorry for her.

Slade dropped his cigarette butt to the dirt and carelessly ground it with a boot heel. "Not this time, darlin'," he drawled. "Maybe I'll take a rain check." Tipping his hat to Allie and completely ignoring Pete, he strode toward his truck and gunned the engine. It was only after he'd rounded her long driveway that she noticed his smashed cigarette lay in the freshly turned soil of her rose garden.

Chagrin and a great longing mingled on Tricia's face. Pete's expression was hard and knowing. Allie sighed.

"*I* won't take a rain check." Pete bit out his words as he addressed Tricia. "Mind you don't burn the bread." Before she could react, he headed for the barn, shoulders squared and head up.

Carefully Allie began clipping again. "You know, Trish," she said, "a smart girl can recognize the type of man that'll be true to her. And she can spot a womanizer a mile off. Slade's not looking for anything lasting."

Shrugging with massive teenage unconcern, Tricia started up the steps. "I know Slade dates a lot. He just hasn't found anyone who really cares for him. That's all he needs to settle him down."

Allie tried not to groan. "That may be so," she allowed. "But his track record isn't good. I personally know of three women who've had their hearts broken, or near to it, by Slade. They all cared for him."

"They weren't the *right* woman," Tricia insisted.

"But wouldn't it be smarter to go for a steady man? Someone a woman can rely on—someone willing to offer his heart in return for hers?" She paused and glanced at the barn. Softly she said, "Pete's sweet on you. And he's growing into a wonderful man."

"Pete's all right, I guess," Tricia said. "But he's... *boring*. Slade's exciting. Besides, you should talk. You're half in love with Dal, and he's not such a good choice. He'll be taking off in no time."

Stunned, Allie felt the blood drain from her face. Was it so obvious? Struggling, she searched for a reply but none came to mind. She hadn't expected her advice to be thrown back at her.

How had she become such a hypocrite? Who did she think she was, advising Tricia, when she, herself, was probably the one in most need of it?

Allie tried ignoring Dal, tried not allowing herself to think about him. He was not suitable for her, so she'd best put him in the same category as she would any other employee. Around her heart she would build an impenetrable wall of reserve.

At lunch she went about serving the men and knew she was quieter than normal. Keeping her eyes from meeting his, keeping her distance, she put her new plan into action. As sensitive as Dal was to her moods, she knew he noticed because she saw him send her several questioning glances. It was just too bad, she told herself, if he was puzzled. He'd get used to it.

She concentrated so hard on ignoring him she barely heard the talk until something caught her attention.

"He got throwed so high he coulda said his prayers before he lit," Josh finished, brandishing his spoonful of stew into the air.

"Who got thrown?" Allie said sharply.

Josh opened his eyes wide at her tone. "I just finished saying—Dal did. Offa that cuttin' horse he was riding. Seems that buckskin didn't want to work no cows. Why, when Dal lit in the dirt, that horse hoofed it mighty fast for the high country. We had a heck of a time catching him."

With an injured tone, Dal announced indignantly, "I wasn't thrown! I was right with that bronc, but when I started to fan him, I lost my hat. I just had to get off to look for it."

Josh and the others roared in disbelief and Dal grinned.

"Are you hurt?" Allie asked Dal with what she thought was admirable professionalism. Naturally it was her duty to inquire about the health of her hands. Her eyes went over every inch of him with painstaking care.

He shrugged ruefully. "Naw, I'm all right. Got a sore side and shoulder." He rubbed it for a moment. "But when that horse started pitching unexpectedly and got kinda close to that little creek that runs in the west pasture, damned if I didn't think I was in for a bath. And hell, it isn't even Saturday!"

The others continued laughing, and Allie permitted herself a small smile. Anyone who rode horses as much as these men were bound to get thrown now and again. It meant no loss of face and came with the territory. "I'll have a look at you later," she told him. It would be no problem for her to run probing fingers over his naked muscular shoulder, she swore to herself. It would not affect her in the least.

He caught at her waist as she passed by, her hands full of plates. "I'd like that."

At the feel of his big hands on her sensitive spine, her breath caught, but she glared her disapproval at him. He would have to understand that touching between them now was forbidden!

Jessie helped not at all by sleepily coming into the kitchen just then from her bedroom and climbing into Dal's lap. Allie tried not to glare at Jessie, too, the traitor.

Conversation resumed, more stories about the cattle work were told, and as Allie poured coffee, she noticed Dal whisper something into Jessie's ear. She nodded once, and got off his lap to open the refrigerator and extract a bottle of cola. She gave it to Dal with a smile and he unobtrusively dug into his jeans.

Allie had to strain from her vantage to see past four of the men's heads to tell what he was doing. Then she caught the glint of coins passing from Dal's callused fist to Jessie's small palm. The girl's tiny fingers closed around the money in delight, and when she ran off, Allie knew she was going to deposit them into her piggy bank.

His head bent away from her, Dal couldn't possibly know if Allie had observed her watching him. He hadn't done it to impress her—or gain favor. He'd done it for Jessie. Judging by the growing weight of the piggy bank on Jessie's dresser, he'd given her coins often.

Allie sighed and swallowed hard. Totally unexpected tears started behind her lids and she faced the sink quickly to hide them. How was she to resist a man who treated her beloved daughter with such respect and affection? How was she to refrain from admiring his strong frame when she knew he wasn't looking?

While all the men were still there after lunch, she had Dal sit on the easy chair, unbutton his shirt and pull it off his sore shoulder. When a large purple bruise was revealed, she gasped.

Josh Barnett sauntered over to have a look. "That's a beaut," he remarked. "Got just such a mark myself a few years back. Was ridin' a mean old gelding named Inferno—"

"*You* weren't ever thrown," Dal said to him with mock certainty. "Not *the* Joshua Samuel Barnett of Lubbock, Texas, the best bronc peeler west of the Mississippi!"

Josh shrugged, smiling. "Yeah, well, it was in my younger, greener days. Nobody coulda stayed on that gelding. That horse could buck off a man's whiskers." He shook his head, remembering.

Allie smiled and without thinking touched Dal's hard cheek. "Well, Dal's still got his."

When he twisted to look at her, a new warmth in his gaze, suddenly she realized what she'd done. Briskly she told him,

"Turn around, will you? How am I supposed to check the damage if you're facing me?"

"Sorry." Obliging her, he presented her with his back again. Josh ambled over to where the other men were enjoying a last cup of coffee.

Since Dal had only pulled his shirt half off, it would be necessary for her to remove it completely, she decided, seeing the nasty purplish color extending down his side. When he waited, she gathered courage. Touching him meant intimacy, exactly what she wanted to avoid. But if she backed down now, the men would wonder.

After several seconds she tugged gingerly at his shirt-sleeve, careful not to touch his skin, which was silly, because in order to examine the wound, she would have to. Touch him.

Dal sat patiently, elbows on knees, head bent. Hatless, his thick hair was mashed a bit from a day under the Stetson. She noticed it was getting longish in the back; he needed a cut. She had a good pair of shears. Should she offer?

From the darkly tanned area at the back of his neck, the skin abruptly changed hue where the sun never hit. Hours of the physical labor of hefting hay bales, stringing fence and wrasseling steers had built his biceps into swells of muscle and had carved grooves of taut sinew down his forearms. Allie thought of the times his strong arms had embraced her, and her breath caught in her throat.

Even as she fought for air, he shifted his elbows, and she caught a glimpse of his furry chest that disappeared into his belted work jeans. He wore no trophy ornament, as she did, but a plain silver clasp buckled at his abdomen. Her eyes wandered lower.

"Maybe if you rub salve into it, it'll help," Dal suggested, keeping his head down.

"Oh," she said, her mind jerking back to the task at hand. "Your, uh . . . back?"

He cocked his head to give her an enigmatic smile. "What else?"

Hating herself, she dropped her gaze and swallowed. Trying for convincing bravado, she said, "If you think any ribs are cracked, I'll have to tape them." With probing fingers, she pressed her flattened palm over each rib. She rested her other hand on the warm smooth skin of his shoulder. "Does this hurt? Or this?"

He grunted when she probed a lower rib. In softer tones he said, "Much as I like your hands on me, honey, I'd just as soon you put them elsewhere right now."

Allie straightened, her hands dropping away, her expression stiff. "Nothing's broken, or you'd do more than complain—you'd yell when I pressed down. Do you think you'll be able to continue work?"

He looked startled at that. "Hell, yes. It'd take more than a little spill off that buckskin to keep me down." He shrugged back into his shirt and stuffed the tails into his jeans. When he neglected to rebutton it all the way up, she had to resist the urge to reach out and do it for him. It was a small loving chore a wife might do for her man.

But she wasn't his wife. And he wasn't her man.

She moved toward the kitchen then, surprised to see Josh and one or two of the others eyeing her speculatively. Had she done anything out of line? Inadvertently revealed her strong attraction for Dal?

The men began getting to their feet, collecting their hats, taking last sips of coffee, but no one said anything to her about it. That, in itself, was unusual. Great teasers, the cowboys normally would jump on her with good-natured razzing if they suspected she was sweet on one of them.

Allie studied their faces, but received nothing but bland smiles and polite thank-yous. Watching them file out for afternoon work, she wondered if she still held her secret.

Was there a way, she asked herself without hope, of hiding such a thing?

After the roundup was over, Dal advised Allie to sell a number of her older cows to packer houses, and some of the calves to feedlots. She quickly complied, knowing his expertise surpassed her own. In this way, he explained as the trucks came to collect the cattle, she'd have some extra money for the upkeep of the ranch until the fall sale.

"That account of yours is getting mighty low after paying off the men," he remarked, slapping one fat cow on the rump to get it into the chute. "You could use a cushion. There'll be enough to get some stout fence posts and fencing for that section along Hunt's land. Pete and I can string it this week."

"Good." Allie tried to keep her smile small and impersonal, despite her pleasure at his words. This was business, after all. Dal was merely doing his job.

"And," he touched her nose with a finger, "I've got another project in mind."

She carefully moved back half a foot. "What is it?"

"You'll see." He strode away in a jingle of spurs, daring her to question him.

Before she could decide what to do, a Lubbock Feed Barn truck pulled into the drive, Tricia behind the wheel. Allie was surprised. "Trish, it's nice to see you, but I didn't need you today."

"I know." The girl jumped down, for once wearing smart, lizard-skin cowboy boots instead of pumps. "I'm delivering the paint you ordered."

"But I didn't—"

"I ordered it," Dal broke in, already lifting several gallon cans from the back of the flatbed. "Tricia's dad had it stashed in the back of the feed barn and agreed to sell it for wholesale price. Now you'll get your barn painted, like you wanted.''

"Wholesale price?" Allie was delighted. Mentally she tallied up the cost and decided the amount might not drastically reduce her new savings.

"It's okay," Dal said, apparently reading her mind. "It's in the budget. And the place needs sprucing up. I also had these two-by-fours sent out to replace the rotting boards on the roof. We don't want any wet hay next winter, eh?" He winked at her and she smiled, despite her resolve.

It had long been her hope to return the ranch to its former shape, and Dal knew it. And his wording implied he'd still be there come winter. Against her better judgment, Allie took new hope.

"Okay." She struggled against the urge to hug him. "I'll do the painting."

He thought about that for a moment. "You can help," he replied, as if the decision was his alone. Strangely, she didn't mind his assumption of authority.

Jessie burst out of the house wearing a pink frilly dress, pigtails flying. "Are you gonna paint, Dal? Can I help? Can I?"

"Sure thing, little tumblebug," Dal said, handing her an armful of brushes. "We'll start tomorrow. But you'd better wear old clothes. You don't want paint on that pretty dress."

Jessie looked at him solemnly. "I won't get any paint on it."

Chuckling, Dal grinned at Allie over Jessie's head. "But you will wear old clothes, won't you? For me?"

The girl considered that. "Okay. If you want me to."

Allie eyed her daughter with a mixture of rueful tolerance. *You'd do anything he asked,* she accused the four-year-old mentally. *Just like me.*

Across the yard Pete waved off the cattle truck, and Allie saw him catch sight of Tricia. Briefly his expression brightened. Dal crossed to Pete, said something low to the young man, then slapped him on the back. They both turned to look at Tricia.

Pete nodded slowly, glanced away from the girl, then back again. After a moment his face masked into a frown of concentration.

Allie had a moment to wonder what Dal had told him. Pete called to Allie, "I'll be back to help in a minute. I just want to check on that new calf." Without acknowledging Tricia at all, he disappeared into the barn.

"New calf?" Tricia asked. "I thought your cows had dropped all their calves by now."

Allie grimaced. "So did we. But Pete found this last cow in the farthest section of the ranch, one we missed at roundup, and brought her in. She had the baby last night."

"Oh, could I see it?" Tricia surprised her by asking.

"Help yourself," Allie said. "They're in the barn." She lifted two gallons of paint and followed Tricia into the building.

As she stacked her cans and arranged the painting supplies, she watched Tricia lean over the stall and coo to the newborn calf. Pete knelt in the straw, stroking the baby. "Oh, you darling," Tricia exclaimed to the animal. "What beautiful eyes, so big and brown."

Pete said nothing.

"Were you there when the baby was born?" Tricia asked him.

He didn't look up. Shrugging, he said, "Sure."

Looking at him curiously, Tricia paused a moment. "Even though I've been around ranches all my life, I still haven't seen a calving. How was it to watch?" Tricia waited expectantly for Pete to answer, and Allie paused in her work to observe.

After a long moment, Pete answered reluctantly. "It was okay."

Allie noticed he still hadn't met Tricia's eyes, and she wondered at him. Had he finally been rebuffed by the girl so many times he would no longer try? The scene moments before of Dal whispering something to him returned to Allie.

"I'm wearing boots today," Tricia said suddenly, presenting her footwear beneath the stall door. "Do you like them?"

Over Tricia's shoulder Allie saw Pete's eyes dart once to the girl's feet. "Where's your pointy-heeled shoes?"

The girl shrugged. "I still have them. But I figure they're silly to wear around a ranch. So? Do you like them or not?"

Cautiously Pete raised his gaze to meet hers. He blinked at her smile, then slowly smiled himself. But he didn't blush, Allie noticed. "They're real nice, Trish. Real nice." Getting to his feet, he opened the stall door and let himself out. "Gotta get back to work now," he tossed over his shoulder. "See you around."

Staring after him with comical surprise, Tricia watched as he disappeared out the barn doors and went to work outside. It was the first time he'd actually walked away from her, Allie realized, secretly delighted with Pete's behavior. Maybe if Tricia didn't think she had him under her thumb, she'd recognize the gem he was.

It was hard, sweaty work in the sun, but within three days the barn sported a new coat of soft brown paint, the windows trimmed in white, to match the house. Allie stood well back, swiping a hand across her perspiring brow, proudly surveying the gleaming building.

"She looks brand spankin' new," Dal observed, coming up behind her. He'd painted alongside Pete from dawn to dark, uncomplaining about the uncowboylike nature of the work. Allie marveled anew at his energy. She'd even mentioned something about his not being a "painter," but he'd merely chuckled. "Whatever it takes, darlin', to get the job done. Whatever it takes."

Now he stood behind Allie's shoulder. She could feel his body heat through her sleeveless butter-yellow top—and the pleasant companionship she often felt with him hummed through her. "It's the most beautiful barn I've ever seen." She sighed. "I feel better about the ranch than I have in a long time. I think my parents would be proud. With that fencing you and Pete are going to string it'll be almost perfect."

"Almost?" He cocked a brow. She knew he was proud of the work, too.

But she wouldn't bring up the only thing lacking—replacement heifers—new blood for her aging herd. It was the last big-dollar item she needed to feel completely secure. Allie smiled and said lightly, "Well, perfect would be boring, wouldn't it?"

"No. Perfect would be perfect." He swung around to face the road as the rumble of several large stock trailers sounded on the gravel drive. "Ah, perfection has arrived."

Allie blinked at the spectacle of the trailers wheeling forward. In the back she could see dozens of horned heads. "Cattle?" she said. "What—how?"

"Heifers," Dal supplied with great satisfaction. "It's about time." He started off to confer with the lead driver.

Trying to make sense of the scene, she uprooted her feet and raced after him. "What are they doing here? I can't afford them, Dal. Surely you know that. There isn't enough left—"

"It's okay, Allie," he told her calmly. "I've taken care of it." He resumed walking toward the driver who held a clipboard.

Unease swirled in Allie's stomach as she watched him check the invoice. How had he "taken care" of this, she wanted to scream? She'd suspected there was money in his past—but he had none now—had he? Where had he gotten it?

"Dal!" Desperately trying to keep her voice at a reasonable level, she snatched the clipboard from his hands and gasped at the printed amount. "Dal, what is in your mind? This is impossible!" To the driver she tried, unsuccessfully, to keep the tremor from her voice. "I'm sorry, but they'll all have to go back. There's been a mistake—"

"No mistake." Dal retrieved the invoice from her nerveless fingers, signed it and nodded to the driver. "I told you, Allie, it's been taken care of—and not out of your account. I, uh, handled the payment myself."

"But...how?"

Paying her no attention, he clambered up the high side of each trailer and carefully looked over the stock. "They look great—just what I wanted. We couldn't have gotten a better bunch if we'd gone to an auction."

Watching him, Allie felt her unease heighten. She bit down on the inside of her lip, worrying it. Dal had paid for these cattle? But he had no money, nothing of value save his clothes, his rigging and his horse.

His horse.

Allie paled. Suspicion heavy in her heart, she whirled and ran full tilt for the horse pasture. Because of the barn painting, they'd let the horses run free, and she hadn't paid attention to them for three days, ever since the spring calves had been shipped out.

She ran, and it was hard going in her heavy work boots through the gravel, but she couldn't slow down. Perspiration broke into beads on her forehead, upper lip and beneath her arms, but she didn't care.

At last she came to the split-rail fence surrounding the horse pasture and climbed to the top rung. With her hand, she shaded her eyes and squinted at the small group of animals calmly swishing away flies beneath a stumpy cottonwood.

There was the buckskin Dal had been thrown off, the chestnut Pete favored, her own mare and several others. But nowhere to be seen was the glistening, night-dark coat of ebony she had come to associate only with Dal.

Black Jack was gone.

Chapter Nine

Shock, wonder and awe spiraled through Allie as she leaned heavily on the split-rail fence of the horse pasture. Dal had sold Black Jack to pay for fence posts and new heifers. For her ranch. For her.

It seemed an incredible and unlikely thing. Cowboys *never* sold their favorite mounts. She wouldn't have guessed him capable of such sacrifice. And yet, he had sold his prized black gelding because she needed the money to upgrade her stock.

Even more shocking was the fact that he owed her nothing. They were not related in any way, indeed, had only known each other a few short months.

Why, Dal? Allie whispered to herself. Why would he make such a giving gesture? For several moments she watched the small herd of saddle horses and let the breeze cool the drying perspiration on the back of her neck. In light of his constant reminders that he would leave, she could not fathom it.

Suddenly the awe she'd felt moments before took over and spread through her like sweet honey. Dal might not admit to feeling much for her—he might not *say* it—but he certainly showed it. In spades. Allie smiled to herself and tilted her face toward the sun. Dal was acting like a man in love.

Within minutes, Allie's suspicion that Dal loved her veered wildly from great certainty to overwhelming doubt. When she confronted him about selling Black Jack for the heifers, he merely shrugged as if bored, and offhandedly said something about the gelding giving him trouble lately. "Besides," he threw out while directing the unloading of the heifers, "I was gonna sell him pretty soon, anyway. A man gets tired of the same horse. I'll take the buckskin, all right?"

Allie gaped. "The buckskin is yours, of course. But he isn't worth a quarter as much as Black Jack. What I can't understand is why you—

Several horned heads rushed down the truck ramp and into a pen, and Allie jumped back from the rails.

"You'd best move away, honey, so I can get my work done." Dal slammed the trailer's tailgate and secured it with a chain. "Just don't let any crazy ideas start in your head. My daddy taught me that when a job needs doing, just do it and don't complain. Your ranch needed a few things to see it'll run at a healthy profit, so I took care of them. That's all." He faced her, brows drawn closed. "That's all," he repeated. "Got it?"

She couldn't have missed his meaning any more than she could have missed the rising of the morning sun. He was warning her not to jump to any conclusions. Nodding once, she studied him solemnly, no longer as certain of his feelings for her.

At dinner all went normally, with no talk whatsoever of Black Jack's sale, or to whom he'd been sold. Allie could tell it was the way Dal wanted it. She said nothing. But each time she looked at him, the desire to question him about his earlier life grew stronger.

The following day Allie finally got a chance to ask some of her questions. At noon she found Dal returning from the west pasture where he'd taken a small herd of the new heifers. Before him, he drove a large cow, a bawling calf at her side.

Though the animal had been dehorned, she was still impressive in size, especially for a Hereford, and must have tipped the scales at well over a thousand pounds. She kept trying to evade the horse and rider, but each time, Dal and his buckskin skillfully turned her back toward the ranch. When they got closer, Allie noticed the cow's left side was swollen. She studied the cow, worried.

Dal reined in. "Looks like frothy bloat—probably from too much green plants. That new alfalfa you put in, the one that's so resistant to winter-killing, unfortunately also contains more sugars. This mama just walked right through that old barbed wire fencing and ate her fill."

Immediately inside the small pen, the sick cow lay down with a groan. Her calf stood at her side, nudging her with his small nose and sending up more pitiful bawling. Dal dismounted quickly. "I'm going to start treatment. If we wait for the vet, she'll be a goner for sure."

Allie hated the thought of losing the cow. "But what are you going to do?"

"Gonna drench her. Can you go to the house and bring out some warm milk?" He forced the cow to her feet by pulling on her tail. When she was up, he quickly hobbled her front legs. It was lucky, Allie thought as she raced into the kitchen, that this particular cow appeared to be very gentle.

Allie hurried back to the pen carrying a pint of warmed milk. "Drenching" a cow involved forcing her to swallow a special remedy, and indeed, Dal already had a long, narrow-necked soda bottle into which he was pouring a meas-

ure of turpentine. Without a word, he took the milk and
poured about half of it into the bottle of turpentine. That
mixed, he fitted an eight-inch piece of soft plastic hose onto
the end.

"Come on, old girl," he soothed the restive cow. "Drink
up." At her side he tied her close to a stout post and took a
firm hold of her big head. Inserting the hose along her
gums, he tilted it up. The cow fought and chewed and finally swallowed while her calf paced and bawled. Dal continued treatment and Allie stuck a hand through the rails to
stroke the cow's gullet. She'd seen veterinarians do this to
stimulate the swallowing reflex.

Pouring one shot at a time, Dal gave the cow time to in-
gest all the strange liquid. Allie could only marvel at Dal's
skill. Drenching was something she'd never try on her
own—it was a procedure that took skill. A cow could
breathe at the wrong instant and she could go down with
fluid in her lungs.

"I've heard of different treatments," she remarked,
gratified to see the cow spilled only a small amount of the
liquid, "but *turpentine?*"

"Yeah." Dal shrugged, smiling as he stepped back. "It's
an old farmer's home remedy. But it works. You see, with
frothy bloat, we need to break up the surface tension of the
rumen liquid so the bubbles are broken down and gas is
freed—"

"Never mind." Allie held up a hand. "I'll trust you. But
tell me one thing. How *do* you know so much about animals?" Reaching through the rails again, this time she
grabbed hold of his arm and held tight. "No, don't turn
away. Don't close up on me, Dal. I won't accept less than
the truth anymore. I want *answers!*"

She watched Dal face her, his surprise at her manner surpassed only by her own. What had compelled her to de-
mand explanations now, of all times?

All she knew was that she was tired of his closed face—tired of the ever-present mystery of his life. She had to *know*.

"Well?" she said, gaining courage as she stared him down. Now that she'd confronted him, she wasn't about to let him off.

"All right." His breath expelled in a short burst and his gaze dropped away from hers. "I'm a veterinarian."

Allie gasped.

"Actually, I *was*. But not anymore. My license has lapsed."

"I should have known." Allie stared at him. "A vet!" So many things fell into place. In fact, the possibility had crossed her mind once or twice, but she'd dismissed it out of hand. Why would a licensed animal doctor work as a cowboy—for mere cowboy wages?

Dal cataloged her predictably changing expressions with a sinking heart. He knew what she was thinking—what she was getting ready to say—and he didn't want to hear. *Dammit.* He never should have told her. Giving a last pat to the cow's flank, he collected the can of turpentine and purposefully headed for the barn.

But Allie wasn't to be deterred. She clambered through the rails, frightening the calf, and chased after Dal. He could hear her trotting up behind him as he set the can on a tack room shelf.

"But, why, Dal? Why don't you have an office somewhere? Or get a full-time job on a big ranch—*use* your degree—instead of letting it go to waste?"

He shrugged, saying nothing.

"It's such a crime. It's so—so stupid!" She was working herself up now, he could hear the urgency build in her voice. In a way, he understood. An infinitely practical woman, she would never see how his professional life was completely intertwined with his private. In that one fateful moment, he'd lost his personal identity—and his professional right along with it.

"Dal," she took hold of his arm again and he stoically let her hang on while he washed his hands in the small cold-water sink. "How did you get to be a vet? Who paid for your schooling? Your parents? Did they have to scrimp and save to put you through? Did they sacrifice so that you could get a degree you don't even use?"

At that he cast her an irritated glance and almost shook off her hold on his arm. But she would only grab on again, he told himself with forbearance. "I don't want to talk about it, Allie," he growled, striking out for the door.

But she rushed past him and barred the way, slender arms outstretched, as if her puny strength could hold him inside. He almost laughed at that.

But one look at her expression, and the desire to laugh expired. Instead of the pleading, angry or downright curious look he expected to see on her face, she wore the determined countenance of a woman on a mission. This time she wasn't to be thwarted.

He halted and rested both fists on his hips. "Look, nobody scrimped to put me through school, all right? And nobody cares whether I use my degree or not." He shrugged. "I got tired of working day in and out at the same place. It was boring, okay? I'd rather earn my way cowboyin'. Now I get to move on when things wear me down."

"No," she countered shrewdly, her pretty eyes narrowing. "That's not all, is it, Dal? I know you fairly well now, and I can tell, you're leaving something out. You're leaving out a *lot*."

He shook his head, his patience wearing thin. Brushing by her as easily as brushing off a horsefly, he stalked outside and began reexamining the sick animal. The cow was standing quietly, allowing her calf to nurse. A good sign.

Allie chased right after him. "Why, Dal?" she insisted. "Why are you throwing it all away?"

"You wouldn't understand," he told her.

"Of course not, when you won't talk to me!"

He said nothing.

"You're right, I *don't* understand," she shouted. Her eyes were wide with fury; her braid swung against her back like the tail of an angry mare. "If I were you I *would* use what I'd worked to attain. But I don't have a college degree—I never gave myself a chance to get one. At nineteen I made the worst mistake of my life and ran off with a boy." Suddenly her voice lowered and her gaze dropped. "Just a boy. He played at being a man."

Dal studied her pinched face. He didn't like having to ignore her. Softly he asked, "Tell me about it."

"Oh, great! You want *me* to talk—but you won't. Well, fine. I'll tell you." Her blue eyes took on a hard, brittle appearance in the harsh sunlight. "I was a model, only child, living in a loving home. I lived to please my parents—got good grades—was sweet to everybody. It was an ideal life. They wanted more kids, you see, but were unable to have them. So I got all their attention, all their love and approval."

"And?"

"And I had just graduated from high school and been accepted to Austin University, and even earned a partial scholarship. My mother and father had saved for years and were going to pay the balance. I hadn't chosen a major yet, I didn't know what I wanted to be or do. So I thought I'd take general courses for a while."

"That was a good idea," he encouraged. He was glad to get her off the subject of himself, even if her confession appeared to be hurting her.

"Yeah. A good idea." The brittle look in her eyes grew even harder. "But one hot August afternoon a group of motorcycle-riding guys rode into Lubbock while I was having a cola at Carson's drug store. My girlfriends and I were so impressed—one young tough even looked like James

Dean. You know the type—leather jacket—hair too long. We girls flirted and giggled and flirted some more.''

Dal stood quietly stroking the cow's throat. "This James Dean character—he the one you were sweet on?"

"Dwight Paxton." She spat out the name. "Oh, I was warned. By friends, by family. But I wouldn't listen. I was so enamored of the sullen way he sat his big Harley and of his bad-boy looks. He even smoked cigarettes—and I hate smoke!" She shook her head, as if still unable to believe it.

"So he made a few promises he didn't keep. It's an old story." Dal forced out the uncaring words; he knew she didn't want pity.

"An old story," she agreed stiffly. "But for me it changed my life forever. You already know the rest. I ran off, gave up my friends and family, even my college scholarship. In two months, when I discovered I was expecting, Paxton said a baby would hold him back."

"Why didn't you go home, Allie? From all accounts your parents were good people. They'd have taken you in."

Anguish twisted her pretty features. "I couldn't!" She whirled toward the barn, lacing her fingers together. "I'd thrown away everything. I'd betrayed my parents' trust. Their hearts were broken by my selfishness. I can still see the shock and hurt on their faces when I told them I was leaving." She swallowed hard. "So when Paxton left, I got a job as a waitress in San Antonio and saved for Jessie's birth. When she came, I went right back to work and didn't come home here until I got the jolt of my life and found out my parents had both died. The executor of their estate tracked me through my employer." She finished on a sob, her thin shoulder quaking.

Dal took a step toward her and put a hand on her shoulder. He admired her courage and the effort it must have taken to have a baby alone, in a strange town. "Allie—"

"No!" She jerked away. "No platitudes, please. What I did was wrong, and I've had to live with it. If I had to do it

over again, I'd do it, just to get Jessie. But I would have returned home—made peace with my parents. They'd have
loved her . . . I know it.''

"I'm sure they would.'' He paused. "You've done a terrific job raising her. Everybody loves Jess.''

"Yes.'' She made a valiant effort and lifted her head.
When she turned to face him, he saw that her eyes were dry,
and he marveled at her strength. "However, I've learned
from my mistakes. I'm back on my family ranch now, and
I'm going to make it work or die trying. I want Jessie to
grow up here and know the rewarding work and wonderful
fun of living on a ranch—like I did. It's all I can do now.''
She said this last softly, and Dal knew her struggle was her
way of making it up to her parents. Softer still, she said,
"But at least I'm not a coward anymore. Not like you.''

An uneasiness growing inside him, Dal began unbuck-
ling the cow's hobbles. He hated himself for asking, "What
do you mean?''

"I'm not afraid anymore, Dal. I've faced the worst and
survived. I'll do 'anything it takes,' your daddy's credo, to
keep this ranch afloat. I'm a fighter now. But you're not.
You're running scared.''

He scowled. They were back to him again. "Think what
you want.''

He moved to untie the cow's halter rope when Allie said,
"You could be a fighter, too.''

An unwilling grimace passed over his face. "I've faced
plenty in my life, boss lady. There isn't anything or anyone
I'm scared of.''

With a gentleness that ate at his patience, Allie suggested, "You're a man at war with yourself. You're your
own worst enemy. And you *are* frightened. One thing
frightens you more than anything in the world.''

"Yeah?'' Mounting anger made his words curt. While she
was talking about herself, he didn't mind, but come to *his*
business, and that was getting too close to home. "I've

about had a belly full of your amateur counseling. But just for conversation's sake, tell me. What's this *thing* I'm supposed to be so terrified of?''

"I don't know exactly."

He let out a triumphant guffaw and began leading the cow away.

"It's something from your home."

Four feet away he stopped but didn't turn. "I don't have a home."

"We all hail from somewhere, as much as we try to run away. Or is this thing you want to escape . . . *someone?* Perhaps several people. Tell me when I'm getting warm."

All at once Dal tired of his own prevarication, tired of the agony locked inside. The escalating anger inside him quieted, leaving him feeling drained. The hard years of loneliness suddenly seemed to weigh down on his back, bending his strength. "You're warm, all right." Slowly he met her eyes over his shoulder. "But you're wrong about going back. In my case it's impossible. It can't be done."

"It can!" She leapt forward, startling the cow so much that the animal broke free of Dal's lead rope and trotted off. Allie hardly noticed. "Oh, Dal, don't make the same mistake I did and wait until it's too late."

He shook his head.

"For your own sake, for your *soul*—go back and make good. I have faith in you, Dal whatever-your-name-is. Don't tell me your last name. I don't care anymore. All I know is that you're a *good* man. A fine person. Whatever you've done can be corrected . . . forgiven. But you've got to try. Try, Dal."

"Maybe. Maybe." He nodded at her; for an instant his heart lightened. Her faith and enthusiasm made it seem possible. Perhaps he *could* return home and repair the damage. Maybe he could.

Just as instantly he knew he wouldn't consider it. He'd already thought about going home so many times he was sick of it. At some point in the past two years he'd closed the door on that portion of his life. It was a door bricked shut, hopeless to open.

Catching up the reins of his ground-tied buckskin, he put one foot in the stirrup, swung up and set out after the cow to push her and her calf into a nearby observation pen. Behind him he felt Allie watching, one hand at her mouth as if she wanted to say more. With a touch of his spurs, he nudged the gelding into a slow lope and set out to do the work he figured was meant for him.

Slade stopped by that very afternoon, catching Allie admiring her newly painted barn from the newly hoed rose patch. Tricia had come out to the ranch, ostensibly to bring a last can of white trim paint, but Allie wondered. Could it be the girl's interests were changing? She seemed a fraction more aware of Pete, ever since he'd started ignoring her.

It was with a musing smile that Allie greeted her neighbor, who roared up in a cloud of swirling dirt. She dusted the soil off her knees and set aside her rose clippers. After greeting Slade, she brought him coffee, and they sat together on the wide porch steps, sipping the steaming brew.

"Barn looks good," Slade allowed. "And there's paint in your hair. You been working, huh?"

"Sure have," she drawled back. Somehow the man didn't seem such a threat as he had at one time. It could be that he'd been nice to her for a long while now. His kindnesses were slowly erasing their stormy childhood relationship.

Or could it be that with Dal on her ranch, she just felt safer? Slade's legendary attraction hardly touched her. She could admire his classic features without feeling any longing for him. The thought made her smile wider.

"You shouldn't work so hard, Allie," Slade said, studying her smile.

"I thrive on it."

"Seems like."

They fell silent, sipping coffee companionably while Allie waited for him to broach the reason for his visit. She figured it would be rude to ask.

At last he said, "You know, we've been neighbors a long time, my family and yours."

"Yep."

"And probably will be for a long time to come."

"Probably."

"Well, I've been thinking. Neighbors should get along, don't you agree? I mean, get along not just in an average sort of way, but well. Real well." Suddenly his lips pulled back in a wolfish grin and Allie marveled at his manner. What could he be up to? She said nothing.

"So, I was hoping you'd accept my apology for that date we had a few weeks back."

"Why, Slade," Allie said, lowering her mug in puzzlement, "there's no apology needed. You were a perfect gentleman."

"Was I?"

"Yes."

"That's a relief." He finished his coffee and let the cup dangle from his fingers. "Because I really respect you. You've done darn well here, and I have to tell you somethin'. When you first came back, I didn't think you'd do so good. Figured you'd pack up after a few months. Sell out."

"Never." She said the word with pride.

"I can see that." Slade smiled at her long and slow, causing her the first twinge of uneasiness. "And now that I can see you're serious about stayin', maybe you and I could work out some sort of... arrangement." With a deliberate movement he dropped a hand to her knee and squeezed.

Uneasiness became suspicion. "Slade," she began carefully, "I hope you aren't suggesting something I wouldn't want to hear."

"Course not! What kind of man do you take me for?" He looked affronted. "But I want to know something. Are you...uh, dating that hired man of yours?"

"Dal? No, we're not...dating." It was certainly true. They hadn't been on a single date.

"That's good." Slade's laughter held a shade of triumph. "That's real good. Didn't think you'd go for that sort of scruffy cowhand, anyway...but I had to make sure. A man's got to know his competition, you understand."

"Slade, I—"

"Now, honey, don't you worry. You and I will do just fine together."

"I'm sure we will," Allie told him with a good bit of caution. "But I've had a lot on my mind lately. I'm afraid I'm not quite sure what you mean."

"Why, I'm talking about you and me, Allie. Call it a...partnership." He looked supremely satisfied with his wording, and he squeezed her leg again.

Allie glanced down at the tanned hand resting on her knee and had the oddest sensation of wrongness. It shouldn't be Slade's hand touching her with such familiarity. A tanned hand, yes. A large, masculine hand—one callused with hard work—and strong. But not Slade's.

Suddenly Allie's patience broke. "Are you asking for my hand in marriage, Slade?"

He couldn't have been more surprised if she'd ripped off her top and jeans and danced naked before him. "Now, honey, surely I didn't say anything to lead you to believe—"

"What are you getting at?" She stared at him without blinking.

"Well, I'm not meant for permanency, you oughta know that. And I tell all the girls the same."

"All the *girls?*" One of her brows arched cynically. "Don't you mean *women?*"

"Sure, sure." He was getting exasperated. "You know what I mean—"

"No, I don't know. Why don't you lay your cards on the table, Slade. Do you mean you want us to live together? Or perhaps just sleep together when it's convenient—say maybe. on Wednesday and Saturday nights—provided it doesn't interfere with your other dates, of course."

Slade muttered a low and earthy expletive. "You'll bene-fit, don't you understand? I'll help you with your ranch. Pay some of the bills—get that little daughter of yours her pony. She wants one real bad, you know. Hell, I'll get her two!"

Mustering her dignity, Allie stood. "As you've said, we've been neighbors a long while. And will be for a long time to come. So far we've gotten along just fine. Let's keep it that way."

Surprise slackened Slade's handsome features as he looked up at her. "You mean you don't want—"

"I'm afraid not." She shook her head and smiled coolly.

After a long moment he smiled back, albeit reluctantly. "Not interested, huh?"

"Not interested."

An instant later, his arrogant grin back in place, he got to his feet. "That's too bad. Our ranches together would be some spread. Maybe later you'll think about selling."

"No."

"Okay. It's just that things are going well for you now. And don't misunderstand—I'm glad. But come a harsh winter, you may decide—"

"No, Slade."

He presented his palms. "All right. All right. You don't have to get out your shotgun." Tipping his hat, he jogged down the steps muttering something that sounded like, "Can't say I didn't try."

Tight-lipped, Allie watched him walk toward his truck. She didn't suppose he'd been turned down by many, and it made her proud she'd been one of the few who had. Fortunately he'd given in fairly easily, as if he hadn't really expected her to go for his...*arrangement.* As determined as she was to hang on to her family ranch, as desperate as she was to keep it, she couldn't pay Slade's price.

As she watched, Tricia came out of the barn, wearing her usual tight jeans but again with sensible Western boots. Her nose was pressed into the soft fur of two new calico kittens she held in her arms. When she spotted Slade, her steps faltered.

He saw her at the same moment and turned on his heels to intercept her. They were just out of earshot but Allie worried about what he might be saying.

Casual flirting was the most Slade had ever indulged in with the teenaged Tricia. He hadn't taken her girlish crush seriously, preferring to tease her and brush her off.

But as Allie watched, he stood over Tricia, scratching the kittens under their chins, then softly caressing Tricia in the same place. Even from her vantage across the yard, Allie could see the confused pleasure on the girl's face. Slade cupped her cheek, ran his hand down her hair and rested it on her shoulder.

Darn that man, Allie swore inwardly, her hands curling into fists. *Damn* the low-down snake for taking advantage of the impressionable girl. If he couldn't get the woman rancher, why not go for easier pickings, the feed barn owner's daughter?

Suddenly, in Slade, Allie saw Dwight Paxton. A selfish male animal intent on satisfying his own sexual needs, without more than token concern for the female. But worse, in Trish, Allie saw herself. Young. Vulnerable. Easily led astray. Easily abandoned.

Could she interfere? Should she? How often she'd warned Tricia, counseled her against falling for Slade Hunt. All had fallen on deaf ears. Six years ago her own ears had had selective hearing when it came to Dwight Paxton. Allie sighed, seeing the shy smile on Tricia's upturned face.

And she *was* eighteen, legally an adult, however much Allie tended to think of her as a mere girl. It was difficult, though, watching Tricia head down the same certain path of pain she, herself, had trod.

Just before dinnertime Dal sent word through Pete he would be working late digging out a bogged water hole in the east pasture. Tricia stayed on, however, and helped cook up a pot of chili. Since the chili was too spicy for Jessie, the girl ate chicken soup, then settled down to watch her favorite afternoon cartoon.

Allie and Pete and Tricia sat to eat, and Allie noticed Pete gave Tricia little attention. Carefully she announced, "Slade came by again today."

Pete glanced up sharply. His mouth was half-full of chili. "What'd he want?"

Allie shrugged. "He asked if I'd, uh...date him."

Frowning, Pete swallowed, looked as if he would speak, then changed his mind and stuffed another huge spoonful of chili into his mouth.

Tricia's silence was noticeable. With exacting concentration, she spread butter on a roll.

"You gonna date him, Allie?" Pete asked.

She looked straight at Tricia. "I don't believe so. But I want you to know, Trish, that if you want to, I won't stand in the way. I was out of line, warning you off him. It's none of my business. Besides, you're a big girl now. You can make your own decisions."

With a nervous flick of her eyes, the teenager glanced at the boy across the table. Weakly she replied, "Thanks."

"It's nothing." Allie pushed the plate of bread toward Pete. Interesting. Not long ago the girl would have jumped at the offer. By withdrawing his affection, had Pete made Tricia notice him? Maybe even appreciate him? Allie watched his frown deepen and his hand form a fist around his spoon. She said, "Want a roll, Pete?"

"No! I mean…no, thank you." He stared at Tricia, then so suddenly it startled her, he stood, almost knocking his chair over backward. Shooting out a hand, he caught and righted it. With his other hand he reached for his baseball cap and jammed it on his head. "I've had enough."

In six strides he was out the door, banging it behind him. Innocently Allie looked at Tricia. "Gosh, what's gotten into him?"

One side of the girl's mouth rose in a weak attempt at a smile. Her gaze had dropped to the tablecloth. If Allie didn't know better, she'd guess Tricia was ashamed of herself. "I don't know."

"Well, it looks like nobody's got much of an appetite today. I'd best get the dishes washed."

"I'll wash." Tricia got to her feet and hurried to the kitchen sink. Coincidentally the window over the sink had a clear view of the yard. Outside, Pete mounted his horse and spurred him into a gallop. Tricia craned to watch, and then her shoulders slumped. Dishes in her hands, Allie pursed her lips.

Dal bent into the small bunkhouse refrigerator and snagged a can of lukewarm beer. The fridge didn't work so well; it was old, the wiring shorting out more often than it connected. But it kept the beer slightly cooler than the rest of the room, and for small favors, he'd learned to be grateful.

Dropping into one of the cane-backed chairs before the small wooden table, Dal tugged and let one dusty boot drop, then the other. The beer poured down his throat in a cool rush, satisfying a transitory need. One elbow he rested on the chair, the other on the table, the can dangling limply from his fingers. Neither beer nor anything else could satisfy the permanent ache inside. An ache that had grown with time, instead of lessened.

At least now he fully understood Allie's motives as she fought desperately for the ranch's solvency. He admired her tenacity, her perseverance. She was a woman who knew what she wanted and would do much to get it. Unfortunately, because of this single-mindedness, she couldn't savvy anyone else who didn't have clear-cut goals. She didn't understand *him*.

Hell, did it matter? Dal got up, crushed the empty can in his fist and hurled it at a full trash can. It banked on the rim and hovered for a second. Then it fell on the scarred wood floor. A few remaining drops of beer spilled and Dal stared at them morosely. After a second he whirled, leaving the can alone, and threw himself onto his bunk.

It was getting dark outside, the sun making a final stand on the horizon, the animals in the barn quieting for the coming night. Dal should be quieting, too, but somehow he just couldn't. Wasn't time supposed to heal wounds?

Yet how could it, when that confounded woman reminded him of his past on a daily basis—whether she meant to or not? Allie made him think of things like integrity and pride. Things like tenacity and quiet enjoyment of a task well accomplished. And now that he'd blown it and admitted he'd been a veterinarian, he knew she'd never give him peace.

Dal shifted his weight, and the thin mattress bunched under him, and the rusted springs squealed. He laced his fingers under his head and stared at the ceiling.

She'd called him a coward. *Him.*

Well, she didn't know anything about him. Or very little. But he'd done right by her, by damn. He'd culled her stock, doctored her cattle, strung new fence, painted her barn. Even Black Jack had been sold off to that horse trader one afternoon while she cooked dinner, so that her herd could be built up.

She'd have a chance now. She was a smart woman, hard-working, practical. She'd make it without him. Because that's why he'd accomplished so much here. So she *could* make it without him.

At the thought a bitter taste invaded his mouth, and he suppressed the urge to spit. Even alone in a bunkhouse he had better manners than that. Suddenly the absurdity struck him, and he felt like laughing. He did, but even to his ears the sound held little mirth. He hated the idea of Allie pressing on alone, with only her small daughter for company. Remote from town as it was here, she'd be defenseless against men with less than honorable intentions.

Dal swore long and colorfully, and when he trailed off, he began to wonder at himself. He actually had to fight the fierce urge to stay on, make Allie his own. To do for her— be here for her—love her.

She'd called him a coward. But she'd also called him good.

You're a good man, she'd entreated him. *Whatever you've done can be corrected . . . forgiven.* Her words echoed in his mind, mocking him, making him yearn for that to be true. Making him hope. That was both the curse and the delight Allie had given him. Hope.

Chapter Ten

Dal was gone. Allie stood in the bunkhouse doorway and surveyed the gaping drawers and bare mattress and knew she didn't have to check the buckskin's stall to be sure that Dal had cleared out again. A feeling of déjà vu hit her. The bunkhouse was empty, as it had been the first time he'd left. But there was one major difference. This time he wouldn't be back. Allie knew it as surely as she knew the horses would have to be fed, the cattle checked.

Shoulders slumping, Allie felt her customary energy seep away. With dragging steps she entered and sank onto the hardwood chair, knees pressed together, fingers tightly laced. The room was cold and lifeless without the big cowboy, as was her heart. Never had she experienced such despair, and despair had touched her before.

Letting Dwight Paxton into her life had been a mistake, she'd known it almost from the start. But letting Dal in hadn't. Even though what she knew of him wasn't perfect, even though she could readily catalog his faults, trusting in Dal had not been a bad thing.

At least, it shouldn't have been. He'd left her, without a word, without promises. Allie let out a hollow laugh. She supposed she should thank him for not lying to her. But while he'd been a part of her life, he'd been a positive influence on both her and her daughter. She hated the fact that he'd left. She hated his cowardice. Not for a second did she believe he'd taken her advice and gone home; she had no illusions.

She supposed she'd pushed him out. With her outburst of the day before, calling him names, demanding he *do* something about the anguish that ruled him, she'd forced him to choose between her and his freedom.

Sighing, tears hovering beneath the surface, Allie forced her emotions to remain banked. She had work to do, a child to raise, a ranch to run. She had no time for foolish weeping. Crying was self-indulgent, and she'd already indulged herself enough.

Allie got to her feet and discovered her knees were shaking. Her stomach felt queasy and her throat tight. As she made a last sweeping glance around the barren room of shadows, she wondered, wasn't a broken heart too heavy a price to pay for her faith?

In the house, Allie served her sleepy daughter oatmeal with honey, then dragged out dirty clothes for washing. Later in the yard she bent over her wash basket, hanging laundry. Atop the little knoll Slade favored, he sat his horse, perfectly still. Allie saw him all right, as she always had, and as usual she ignored him. However, gone were the vague feelings of impending danger she usually experienced when his watchful eyes were on her. Now she felt only annoyance, if she cared at all. Didn't the man have anything better to do than ogle her while she hung wet blue jeans?

Suddenly she unbent, her back fence post straight, and faced him. By ignoring Slade, wasn't she also giving him tacit permission to continue? With a calm serenity she rarely knew, she glared at him, her mouth set in a firm line. He was too far away to speak to, but she hoped her disapproval could be clearly interpreted. Why didn't he just ride off—leave her alone? She hated his proposition of the day before, and if he thought to repeat it, she might be tempted, as he'd suggested, to unearth her father's ancient shotgun and blow his fool head off.

For long moments they faced each other. Then, as Allie watched, he slowly reined his horse away, slinking off like a coyote. She nodded to herself, sure he'd gotten the message. From now on she wouldn't ignore or politely refuse his indecent propositions. Now she'd be very, very clear about her position.

She didn't want or need Slade. Even if she *could* consider selling herself to him in exchange for subsidizing her ranch, it wasn't necessary now. All the spring and summer work was completed, except for the haying, which would be easy with some help. From now until next spring, all she'd have to do was maintain. Dal had made sure of that.

At the heels of that thought she had a revelation. Dropping the soggy jeans back into the basket, she stared off into the horizon. She could see it now; how stupid she'd been. All of it, all of Dal's work, ending with the sale of his valuable cow horse, was designed to ensure as much as possible that she *would* make it alone. Dal had never wanted to stay on here, he'd never planned to. Yet he was a good man, as she'd told him, and good men didn't leave women defenseless. So he'd worked and shaped her ranch until it was a sound business concern.

When Pete learned Dal had left, he questioned Allie. While he was shoeing his chestnut that afternoon, she assisted. She tried to be as offhand as possible. "He quit, Pete. I don't know why, exactly. Got tired of working on the same small place, I guess. You know how these cowboys are, greener pastures and all that."

Pete studied her as if he expected more, but Allie found she couldn't say anything else. After a moment she averted her face, afraid he'd see her inner agony. It was terribly difficult, she found, to hold a smile when there was none in her heart.

She handed him another nail. To forestall more questioning, she asked, "Now that you've graduated, have you considered college?"

Easing down the gelding's foot, he straightened, walked around the horse and ran his hand down the animal's other hind leg. Obligingly the chestnut lifted his other foot to be tended. "I'm not crazy about the idea of going back to school," he admitted as Allie handed over a heavy iron file. "But I know I want to continue ranch work. After watching Dal all this time, I think . . . I'd like to try veterinary school."

Allie blinked. "You knew?"

"Sure. It was obvious he knew as much as any vet I've ever seen. Didn't you know?"

"Not really." She half smiled, swallowing miserably. "Dal taught you a lot, didn't he, Pete?"

"He sure did. I wish he hadn't gone and left. Especially without saying goodbye. I would have liked to shake his hand, say thanks."

"Yes." A familiar lump rose in her throat, and she had to fight off a sudden urge to lie down in the hard-packed dirt of the yard and curl into a tight ball of misery. She couldn't exactly tell him that Dal had left without saying goodbye to her, either.

"I've got an uncle in California," Pete carried on, becoming more enthusiastic as he went. "He's on the board of regents of UC Davis. That's a good veterinary college. And my grades have always been good. My uncle says I might have a shot at getting in. Course, I'm too late for this year. But maybe next I'll make it."

Allie found she enjoyed seeing the hopefulness on Pete's friendly face. "I'm glad," she told him, meaning it. "That could be a wonderful career for you. Does this mean you'll treat my animals at a discount?"

"Aw, Allie." Pete grinned. "*Will* I? Is it dangerous to stand in a nest of rattlers with a bare butt?"

With the legacy of the financially healthy ranch Dal had left Allie, she was able to spend more time with Jessie. The hay pasture had been cultivated and seeded and now cut and safely stored in her barn. Even the bloated cow was fully recovered. What else? Her cowboy—the vet—had the magic touch. The prospects of a fine future here were bright; it was everything Allie had worked for, dreamed of, wanted.

She would trade it all for Dal's love.

For four days she carried on, performing her daily tasks, pleased with Pete's work. She and Tricia, always friendly, began to actually *be* friends. When she saw the girl in town, they'd talk about business, the latest clothing fashions, new recipes.

On the fifth day Allie decided she would force herself to take a day off. She would treat Jessie to a small spree of clothes shopping and strawberry ice-cream cones.

In town, nothing was interesting, nothing seemed exciting, even the food she ate was tasteless. For Jessie's sake, she pretended to enjoy the ice cream.

With their few packages and cones dripping in the heat, Allie pulled into the feed barn parking lot and went inside to say hello.

As usual Tricia was behind the counter. A young man in a baseball cap was carefully perusing the silver buckles inside the glass counter case.

"Pete!" Allie said. "I didn't know you were coming to town today. We could have driven in together."

"Oh, hi, Allie. Jess. Didn't know I'd be coming in today, or I would've hitched a ride. Since you gave me the day off, I decided I'd have a look at these buckles." He nodded at the counter.

"I see," Allie said. The buckle he wore was perfectly good. She knew for a fact he'd gotten it for Christmas. At the thought she made a new effort to smile. These days she seemed to see and feel everything through a haze of unhappiness. Handing Jessie over to Pete, he propped the girl on his hip so she could look in the case.

Eyeing his faded cap, Jessie said, "Pete, do you want a real cowboy hat, too?"

"Great idea, Jess," Allie put in. "Maybe a Stetson or a Resistol."

"I don't know." He fingered the bent bill of his cap and grinned sheepishly.

Tricia leaned over the case. "You'd look fine in a dark Stetson, Pete, what with your blond hair and all."

"You think so?"

"Sure. Why not have a look?" She waved at an expanse of wall-hung hats and whispered, "I think I can get daddy to give you a discount."

"Really?"

"Tell you what," Allie said. "If you want, I'll go in for half." When he frowned, she hurried on, "Don't worry, I can afford it. And you deserve a good hat. Make you look more professional when you're roping steers."

When a chocolate brown Stetson hat with a leather band was finally chosen, Allie laid down half of the amount and Pete paid for the other. Tricia rang it up at a reduced price and handed back coins for change. "I saw Slade this morning," she mentioned with great casualness.

"Did you?" Allie put the coins in her purse and made a mental note to drop them, along with some paper money, into Jessie's pony savings. "Did he come in for supplies?"

At her side Pete held his new hat tightly, his gaze hard on the crown.

"No," Tricia said, not looking at Pete. "He wanted to take me to dinner."

Pete went very still.

"I see." Allie drew a deep breath, praying for Pete. "And did you agree?"

Darting a glance at the young man, Tricia moistened her lips and gave a little shrug. "It's funny, but even a month ago I would've killed for a date with that man. But lately I've been watching him. Oh, he's a looker, all right. But he seems to ask all the women out. If one turns him down, he just moves on to the next. Even if one doesn't say no, he eventually moves on, anyway. Know what I mean?"

Allie's answer was full of relief. "Yes."

"And...and a woman wants to feel special. As if she's the only one a man wants. The only one." Although Tricia purported to be speaking to Allie, she had the distinct impression Tricia meant for Pete to hear every word. In fact, Tricia had fixed him with a stare of great solemnity.

"I understand," Allie said softly.

So did Pete. Allie knew that Tricia had always been special to him. A slow grin started at the corners of his lips as he returned her gaze. He looked thrilled.

"I'm off work at six," Tricia offered Pete hesitantly. "Usually I like to go to Carson's for a cola. Do you want to come?"

"I don't know." Pete's happy smile belied his teasing drawl. "Don't much like cola."

"Oh." For once Tricia looked unsure.

"I like coffee."

"They have coffee," she said eagerly.

"In that case," Pete said, "s'pose I could go." In the wall mirror he gingerly lifted the hat to his head and proceeded to cock the brim first over one eye, then the other. At last he settled on pulling it square and low over his forehead. "Like Dal," he said.

Allie's short-lived pleasure vanished. A sharp pain took its place, spearing into her chest and leaving her weak again. For a few minutes she'd been able to forget the mysterious cowboy, for once banish him from where he'd taken up permanent residence, on the surface of her mind.

Now with a single phrase Pete had brought him back, and Allie missed Dal more than ever. Her gaze fell on Tricia. It appeared that she was at last coming to recognize Pete's true value. Holding Jessie so tight the little girl squawked, Allie had to turn away from the others and blink quickly. Why couldn't Dal have thought Allie worthy of him?

She went home. Minutes slowly added up to an hour; an hour gradually built to two, then three, four, eventually twenty-four, until an entire day had passed. Then another. Another. Two weeks dragged by while Allie knew a great draining of her will to carry on. She filled the time with small chores and big ones, playing with Jessie, savoring the sun on her face.

She'd grown to appreciate the smaller joys in life, she supposed, one Sunday afternoon as she sprawled on one of the porch's wicker chairs. Jessie played quietly on the stairs, a plastic horse in each hand. Before, Allie had rushed through each day, hurrying to complete as many tasks as possible, working, always working, seldom taking a moment to enjoy. But now she did.

Allie learned that rushing through every minute produced nothing but a host of hurried minutes, eventually producing nothing but a hurried, wasted life. Dal's laughter and understanding had taught her that. He'd worked long and steadily, but always had a space of time to stop and tease her, kiss her. Even to teach Jessie things. Now Allie closed her eyes and took a sip of her minted ice tea, recalling the time he'd tested Jessie's knowledge of the horse's anatomy.

"What's this?" He'd pointed to Black Jack's foot.

"The hoof," Jessie replied dutifully.

"And this?" His finger rose a few inches.

"Fetlock."

"Good. And this?"

"The...the..." She put a finger in her mouth and grinned up at him engagingly. "I don't know."

"The pastern."

"Pashton."

"Close enough, little tumblebug. Tomorrow we'll learn three new things about the horse, okay?" He wiggled his fingers beneath her chin, tickling her. Allie watched indulgently. Dal was good with Jess.

The scene faded and Allie opened her eyes. Dal and his horse vanished, leaving only Jessie playing alone with her plastic horses. Suddenly Allie had a clear vision of the future: Jess would grow up alone, with no brothers or sisters to play, fight, learn to share with. Allie had been raised in the same way, but she remembered her great longing for a sibling. Her mother had been unable to conceive again, due to complications from her pregnancy. But Allie had had no such complications. She could have other children, if she had a husband.

She never would.

In the past weeks of loneliness and heartbreak, Allie wondered where Dal had gone. Of course, it didn't matter, really. He'd run again. But she knew in her heart that if he'd cared enough for her, he would have stood his ground, fought for the self-esteem and the right to have her.

Dal hadn't cared enough, and that knowledge hurt the most. Overhead, high clouds obscured the sun, casting a pall over the bright sunlight. Setting down her glass of iced tea, Allie slowly lowered her head into her lap and wrapped her arms around her knees. Until now she hadn't cried. She'd missed Dal every minute of every day, but she'd pressed ahead, in her own fashion. Dry-eyed.

Even now she found she couldn't weep. It was ironic, when at last she gave herself permission, the tears wouldn't come, stubbornly held back for so long they now refused.

Had she subconsciously been waiting for him? Gritting her teeth at her stupidity, she curled tighter around her legs, hugging herself, rocking. Inside, the building ache took her breath away. The vast bleakness of her future without him stretched before her in an unending vacuum of pain.

My God, Dal, she cried inwardly, *why couldn't you have loved me?*

Dry, racking sobs lifted her shoulders while Jessie played innocently, steps away.

"Mommy," she cried, "what's that?"

Allie made a supreme effort to rise up until her elbows were on her knees, swallowing repeatedly in a futile effort to diminish the walnut-sized lump in her throat. It wouldn't do for Jessie to see her upset. Her eyes on the porch floorboards, she said, "What's what, sweetheart?"

Jessie pointed one small arm, drawing Allie's gaze out to the long driveway. A dust cloud formed, grew, finally transforming into a sleek white pickup pulling a double horse trailer. The truck and trailer sported smart navy pinstriping running their length, and a half-circle-shaped logo on the side. Allie did not recognize it.

Probably a salesman, or someone who'd lost his way on the country roads, she thought, not really caring. She half stood, prepared to offer directions or a polite refusal to buy anything.

As the vehicle ground to a stop, spraying gravel, Allie noticed that the overhead clouds had moved and she had to squint into the west to see the driver. He climbed out, a big, tall man wearing a night-dark Stetson.

Allie froze and caught her breath.

"Dal!" Jessie flung aside her plastic ponies and raced to him. He caught the girl and swung her in his arms, his smile a brilliant slash of white on his tanned face. When he set her

down, she danced around him. "Dal! Dal! Dal!" she cried
with sheer exuberance.

"Hello, my little cactus flower," he said to her, ruffling
her hair. "Are you still saving for that pony?"

"I got lots and lots of pennies now, Dal! And some bucks,
too!"

"Some bucks, huh? How many?"

"Three!"

"That *is* big dollars. I'm proud." While he spoke the little girl edged around to the back of the trailer and spied the
long tail of a Shetland pony. She squealed, and without another word, raced into the house.

Dal faced Allie from his position at the truck's rear
bumper. "Hi," he said softly.

She couldn't take her eyes off him, nor utter a word. He
wore fresh-creased blue jeans and a red gingham-checked
skirt. His hat was pulled low, in the familiar way Pete had
begun to emulate. He looked wonderful, she thought.
Wonderful.

"Did you—" She licked her lips and tried again. "Did
you win the lottery, or just close the tables in Vegas?"

He grinned, gesturing with a hand at the fancy truck rig.
"You mean these? They're mine. They always have been."

Allie frowned in confusion, but Jessie flew by her with the
force of a tiny cyclone. She ran down the steps, miracu-
lously not falling, and thrust her heavy piggy bank into
Dal's hands.

He weighed it in his hand carefully. With one eye closed,
he screwed up the side of his mouth and said consideringly,
"Yep, I believe this will be just the right amount of pennies
and, uh . . . bucks."

In that moment Allie felt the wide tear in her heart close
a fraction. She carefully held her position on the porch.
Jessie ran to the back of the trailer again and danced foot to
foot as Dal lowered the ramp and backed out a fat spotted
pony. Executing a small bow, he presented the four-year-old

with the haltered lead rope. "Madam," he said, "your mount."

"Can I ride him, Dal?" Jess stroked the soft muzzle. "Can I?"

"Yes, later. But right now you've got to learn how to lead him. Leading a horse is an important thing. Why don't you try it now around the yard here while I talk with your mama?"

"Are you gonna get Black Jack out, too?" she wanted to know.

Black Jack? Allie glanced sharply at the other side of the trailer, and although she could see another horse inside, from her place on the porch she couldn't make it out.

"Er, not yet. First I've got to talk with your mom. Off you go, now." Dal waited until the girl walked away, leading her pony. Then he shifted, fixing Allie with a steady gaze. He nodded at her half-finished ice tea. "Got any more of that?"

"Sure." On shaky legs, she went into the house and fixed his drink. From the kitchen window she saw that he hadn't come up onto the porch, preferring to wait by his bumper, hands thrust into his pockets. He looked, almost, as if he wasn't sure of his reception. Outside she indicated a chair opposite hers. "Would you like to sit down?"

"Thank you."

How polite they were!

As was her way, she said nothing more, preferring to let him take the initiative. He wasted little time.

"Allie, I did as you suggested. I went home."

The glass of tea halfway to her mouth, she stopped. Her voice came out a squeak. "You did?"

"It was good advice. I—I *was* afraid, you were right. I was afraid they all blamed me—hated me."

"They?"

"My sister, my brothers, my father. You see, the man I killed . . . was my sister's husband."

"Good God." Allie felt the shock down to her toes.

He shrugged. "If I could reenact that scene, I would, believe me." He rubbed his brow under his hat and sighed. "I've been over it a thousand times. But, Allie, he had a gun! And he was waving it around. It was dangerous—my sister was pregnant—I had to protect her."

"Of course." She soothed him automatically. It was as natural as breathing, this impulse to reassure the man she loved. Taking one of his hands, she chafed it between her own. "But why would he threaten her?"

"Drinking. Always drinking. But the rest of us didn't know he'd been hitting her. She never told. Hell, we knew the guy drank, but he always seemed good-natured. We didn't know he was violent."

"So then what happened? You struggled for the gun...?" As hard as the admission was on him, Allie could see it was cathartic.

"It went off. The bullet went through his stomach. I couldn't believe it." Pulling his hand away, he covered his face. "There was blood on my hands, my clothes. My sister's screaming has kept me up nights ever since." He looked at her suddenly, eyes anguished. "She shouted at me, called me a murderer."

Allie could barely comprehend it. "I—I've heard of battered wives protecting their husbands, as unbelievable as it sounds. They've been brainwashed into thinking his violence is their fault."

"And then my father arrived, took in the scene, and the shock on his face—I thought he blamed me, too."

"So you ran."

"Yes, as soon as I could." He closed his eyes. "They've been looking for me—my family. But they were searching for a veterinarian practicing under my full name, not a simple working cowboy named just Dal. I didn't want to be found."

"But... why are you telling me all this now?"

He drew in a deep, deep breath. "Because if I'd never met you, if you hadn't forced me to stop turning away from the situation and face it, I might be running still." Slowly he reached across the small space separating them and touched her hand. "I didn't think I'd be accepted home, Allie, or even in the world. Your faith and persistence gave me hope. *You* gave me courage to try."

She couldn't say a word.

"The law had ruled it self-defense—a formality—because the angle of the bullet and the powder burns on his hands told the tale. The gun was registered to him."

"I see."

"But even though I was off the hook legally, in my mind I felt guilty. I'm a man accustomed to *saving* lives, even human ones occasionally, not taking them. It's a terrible thing, to kill someone." For long moments he was silent, then he met her gaze and some of the pain had left his eyes. "My sister—she's getting married again—to one of my best friends. She told me that at the time of the shooting she was hysterical, she didn't mean it. She wants my blessing on her new marriage."

It was difficult to absorb, Dal's story and his sudden reappearance. Especially since she never expected to see him again. But, Lord, was she glad. To give herself a moment, she let her gaze wander over the truck and trailer where Jessie was leading the pony around and around. Something about the half-circle logo caught her eye and she studied it. "What's that mark?" She pointed to the truck.

"The Circle Shell brand, Allie. It's from the Sheldon ranch, out of east Texas."

Slowly she said, "Your last name is Sheldon?"

"Yes. I'm Dallas Sheldon."

"Is that . . . a big ranch?"

When he told her the size and scope of the operation, she exhaled slowly. A spread that large was worth plenty. So Dal wasn't a poor cowboy after all.

Dal's gaze was on her daughter. "Jess looks happy with the pony."

"Is that why you came back? To give it to her?"

"Sure." When he shifted, the sun glinted on the medallion that hung around his neck.

"Now will you tell me about your necklace?"

He shrugged. "My father gave each of my brothers and me a coin to wear when we turned eighteen. Sort of a family tradition. I've told you that part. But people who live in our area occasionally recognize them and know we're Sheldons."

She swallowed convulsively. The medallion was irrelevant. Dal's identity was the most alarming news of all. In the ten minutes since he had reappeared, she'd tried not to hope he might have returned for good. She'd tried and failed. And now, to learn he came from such a well-to-do background killed the burgeoning hope inside.

Her small spread was nothing next to the Circle Shell. Inferior in every way—poor, backward—her ranch's worth was small change for him. This combined with the fact that he admitted the only reason he'd returned was to bring Jess her promised pony ended all her dreams.

Dully she motioned to the trailer rig. "I guess that really does belong to you."

"Yes. But I couldn't use it or any of my family money in the last two years. I didn't feel it was rightfully mine anymore."

She nodded, understanding. If he felt himself an outcast, his inherent integrity wouldn't allow him to touch anything that wasn't his. "You're actually worth quite a lot more than just a fancy rig."

"Yes." Saying no more, he let her think.

"And Black Jack?"

"I sold him to a horse trader with the understanding that the man would first offer him back to my family ranch. But I forbade the trader to reveal my whereabouts. I figured they'd recognize him and buy him. He was waiting for me in his old stall.''

''How nice.'' Even to her ears, her words had a hollow ring. Abruptly she stood, blindly staring at the logo on the trailer. The back of her neck felt tight, her shoulders stiff. ''Well, I suppose I should thank you for coming back to explain all of this. Anyway, I always knew you weren't a murderer.''

He got to his feet and put a hand on her shoulder. ''I know.''

She moved away just enough to be free of his touch. Her composure was wavering, and she was afraid he would see. She hated her weakness—her violent emotions. ''And—and I'll pay you for the pony, of course. It was awfully thoughtful of you to deliver him. Jess is so pleased.''

''Pay me? I don't want your money. The pony's a gift.''

At the rail she gripped it with both hands, leaning some of her suddenly tremendous weight on the old wood. ''Well, fine, then. But at least take the piggy bank. I've been depositing twenties in it. Jess doesn't know, but there's probably close to a hundred dollars inside.''

She could feel his stare on her profile and desperately held on to her poise. In another minute she'd break down, lose whatever dignity she had left. She had to get him out of there. With a sharp movement she turned to him and plastered a polite smile on her lips. ''If there's nothing else, I'd best get back to work—''

''The property behind yours is going up for sale. Did you know that?'' he asked suddenly.

She hesitated, thrown off balance. ''No, I didn't.''

''I don't figure Hunt knows, either, or he'd have scooped it up. But I found out from the county recorder that it's going into foreclosure. Can you afford to buy it?''

She frowned, unsettled. ''You know I can't.''

''But I can,'' he returned gently.

Gaping at him, she said, "You? Why would you want it? Your ranch is hundreds of miles away."

"My family's ranch," he corrected. "Not really mine. I was the resident vet, of course, and I have a one-quarter share ownership. But running it was never the challenge and joy this place is. Too much help from the others, I guess."

He stepped forward, close. So close. Hovering over her, he exuded body heat and she savored it. Along with his physical warmth, she could smell him—lovely familiar scents of alfalfa and leather and horse. Allie closed her eyes painfully, overcome.

He was speaking. At first she could barely hear him. "I like it here, Allie. I want to stay."

"What?" Eyes open, she held her breath.

Gathering himself, he paused, sought her gaze and said, "I want you. And I hope you'll have me." So suddenly it startled her, he scowled, his face growing taut with determination. "And you *will* have me. I'm the only man right for you." Coming forward, he herded her against the railing until they were almost touching. For a brief instant she thought she caught a glimpse of uncertainty in his eyes.

Then from his shirt pocket he produced a black velvet jeweler's box, opened it and held it out. Inside the box a brilliantly sparkling diamond ring, several carats worth, Allie assumed, winked at her.

When she lifted dumbstruck eyes to him, she found he'd gone slightly blurry, as if a thin film had grown over her vision. She opened her mouth, closed it, then tried again. "I—I couldn't possibly put work gloves over such a ring. It's so big and...impractical. However would I wash dishes for all the men, wearing it?" She was blinking rapidly now in a vain attempt to stem a sudden flow of something strange and wonderful. For the first time in years she wept, truly wept, and it felt so good.

"Allie—" Dal closed the gap and crushed her into his arms. He kissed her brow, her jaw, her lips. "Hush. I'm crazy about you, Allison Pearson. Wild about you. I want to live here with you, work here, see this place become a *show* place. I want to help raise Jessie, maybe have more like her. Say you'll let me. Say you need these things, too."

Tears were spilling over now, wetting her cheeks, clogging her throat. She shook her head—what little she could, jammed as it was into his shoulder—unable to take it all in. "No, I can't believe—"

"Don't say no, sweetheart. Say yes. Just . . . yes."

She pulled back an inch, resting her hands on his chest. The ornery cowboy swam before her eyes, but she didn't need any clearer vision to make out the man she adored. "You know I want all those things. You know I want—"

"Me?"

"Yes." She sniffed. "Definitely you."

"Good," he said, smiling wickedly. "I've had a hell of a time getting you to admit it."

"Admit—*I'm* not the one who keeps disappearing. *I'm* not the one who runs away."

"Never again, boss lady," Dal swore. "You couldn't run me off with a stick."

Allie threw back her head and gazed at him with love-filled eyes. "As if I would," she whispered, thrusting her fingers into the hair at the back of his neck and pulling his head down to hers. "As if I would."

*   *   *   *   *

Take 4 bestselling love stories FREE

Plus get a FREE surprise gift!

Special Limited-time Offer

Mail to Silhouette Reader Service™

In the U.S.	In Canada
3010 Walden Avenue	P.O. Box 609
P.O. Box 1867	Fort Erie, Ontario
Buffalo, N.Y. 14269-1867	L2A 5X3

YES! Please send me 4 free Silhouette Romance™ novels and my free surprise gift. Then send me 6 brand-new novels every month, which I will receive months before they appear in bookstores. Bill me at the low price of $2.25* each—a savings of 44¢ apiece off the cover prices. There are no shipping, handling or other hidden costs. I understand that accepting the books and gift places me under no obligation ever to buy any books. I can always return a shipment and cancel at any time. Even if I never buy another book from Silhouette, the 4 free books and the surprise gift are mine to keep forever.

*Offer slightly different in Canada—$2.25 per book plus 69¢ per shipment for delivery. Canadian residents add applicable federal and provincial sales tax. Sales tax applicable in N.Y.

215 BPA ADL9   315 BPA ADMN

Name _____ (PLEASE PRINT)

Address _____ Apt. No. _____

City _____ State/Prov. _____ Zip/Postal Code. _____

This offer is limited to one order per household and not valid to present Silhouette Romance™ subscribers. Terms and prices are subject to change.

SROM-92   © 1990 Harlequin Enterprises Limited

Silhouette
R O M A N C E™

HEARTLAND HOLIDAYS

Christmas bells turn into wedding bells for the Gallagher siblings in Stella Bagwell's *Heartland Holidays* trilogy.

THEIR FIRST THANKSGIVING (#903) in November
Olivia Westcott had once rejected Sam Gallagher's proposal—and in his stubborn pride, he'd refused to hear her reasons why. Now Olivia is back...and it is about time Sam Gallagher listened!

THE BEST CHRISTMAS EVER (#909) in December
Soldier Nick Gallagher had come home to be the best man at his brother's wedding—not to be a groom! But when he met single mother Allison Lee, he knew he'd found his bride.

NEW YEAR'S BABY (#915) in January
Kathleen Gallagher had given up on love and marriage until she came to the rescue of neighbor Ross Douglas . . . and the newborn baby he'd found on his doorstep!

Come celebrate the holidays with Silhouette Romance!

Silhouette CHRISTMAS Stories 1992

Experience the beauty of Yuletide romance with Silhouette Christmas Stories 1992—a collection of heartwarming stories by favorite Silhouette authors.

JONI'S MAGIC by Mary Lynn Baxter
HEARTS OF HOPE by Sondra Stanford
THE NIGHT SANTA CLAUS RETURNED by Marie Ferrarella
BASKET OF LOVE by Jeanne Stephens

Also available this year are three popular early editions of Silhouette Christmas Stories—1986, 1987 and 1988. Look for these and you'll be well on your way to a complete collection of the best in holiday romance.

Plus, as an added bonus, you can receive a FREE keepsake Christmas ornament. Just collect four proofs of purchase from any November or December 1992 Harlequin or Silhouette series novels, or from any Harlequin or Silhouette Christmas collection, and receive a beautiful dated brass Christmas candle ornament.

Mail this certificate along with four (4) proof-of-purchase coupons, plus $1.50 postage and handling (check or money order—do not send cash), payable to Silhouette Books, to: **In the U.S.:** P.O. Box 9057, Buffalo, NY 14269-9057; **In Canada:** P.O. Box 622, Fort Erie, Ontario, L2A 5X3.

ONE PROOF OF PURCHASE

SX92POP

Name: _____

Address: _____

City: _____

State/Province: _____

Zip/Postal Code: _____

093 KAG